The Tipsy Witch
and other
Tairy Fales

The Tipsy Witch
and other
Tairy Fales

by Lewis Meyer

illustrations by
Deanne Hollinger

McGraw-Hill Book Company

New York   St. Louis   San Francisco
Montreal   Toronto

Book designed by Marcy J. Katz

Library of Congress Cataloging in Publication Data

Meyer, Lewis, date
    The tipsy witch and other tairy fales.

    I. Title.
PZ4.M6127Ti [PS3563.E877]   813'.5'4   74–11183
ISBN 0–07–041743–1

   3456789 MUBP 7898765

FOR

ELIZABETH   RENÉE

AND

NATASHA

Contents

Publishers insist on labels. Childrens' stories. Grownups' stories.

But children often act grown-up—and grownups are often childlike.

So how to describe *Tairy Fales*? If a label is absolutely necessary let it say:

These are grownups' stories for children—and vice versa.

L.M.

The Tipsy Witch

The Tipsy Witch

The plane sailed through the sunset into a late October dusk. It was half-full and its passengers half-asleep. The cabin was so quiet that Billy had to concentrate in order to hear the comforting sound of the engines.

Earlier, his grandfather had come into the plane with him and had helped him choose a seat by the window. "You're lucky," Grandfather had said. "You're going to have two seats to yourself." Then, after reassuring the young traveler that his parents would be waiting for him at the Chicago airport in just two hours, Billy's grandfather kissed him good-bye and told him to "watch the lights come on in the cities."

Billy had buckled his seat belt long before being told to. He had waved good-bye to his grandparents, then settled back and waited for the takeoff. The plane had taxied lazily down the runway and stopped. Its big engines had revved and raced and roared. Then, leaving a gale of dust behind it, the plane had sped along the concrete strip and had suddenly begun to climb. With its nose pointed sharply upward, the plane had reminded Billy of a huge bird hurrying home for its supper.

In two hours he'd be home eating his own supper. Afterward, he hoped to have time for a trick-or-treat visit to the neighbors before bedtime. Since Halloween fell on a Saturday this year, his parents had promised to let him stay up an hour longer.

The clouds were marvelous things—fun to sail through. But as the plane climbed higher and higher, the clouds took over the whole sky, and Billy found this exasperating. Even though he pressed his nose against the window, he couldn't see anything except those thick beds of white. First they looked like millions of pillows in clean, white cases; then they resembled billions of snowy mushrooms growing upside down. He knew that there were rivers and farms below him, and cities with their lights coming on, but they were all hidden by this feathery, billowy, tiresome white stuff that wouldn't go away.

Billy used his mental radar and imagined all the wonderful things he couldn't see. He even pretended that the stubborn goo would open suddenly and disclose a flying saucer with red, green, and orange lights flashing brightly while friendly little men inside it waved at him.

Finally, he closed his eyes, hoping that when he opened them the clouds would be gone. He counted to one hundred and one very slowly before peeking, but that did no good. All he saw was the same wing of the same plane and the same monotonous sea of white.

Instead of an exciting jet flight to tell his friends about, here he was, two miles aboveground and bored stiff! He looked at the seat beside him and wished some passenger had taken it so he would have someone to talk to. Even a gabby female like Miss Winters, his fourth-grade teacher, would be better than an empty seat. *Bee-you-ti-ful clouds*, he thought sourly, and he almost said the next word out loud—Phooey!

He'd try one more time. He'd close his eyes and start counting to a hundred and five by fives. Maybe this would change his luck. *Ninety . . . ninety-five . . . one hundred . . . one hundred and five . . .*

He opened his eyes, saw something, didn't believe it, blinked, closed them for a second, looked again, shook his head, then pressed his nose hard against the glass and stared. The clouds were still there, below and all around him. But sitting on the wing of the plane, rubbing her shins, and looking for all the world like a hawk-nosed, angular, skinny, old witch wearing a black, peaked hat *was* a hawk-nosed, angular, skinny, old witch wearing a black, peaked hat.

The witch looked at Billy in a way that said, "What are you staring at? Haven't you ever seen a tired witch before?" Then she continued rubbing her shins.

Billy was shaking. Had anyone else on the plane seen her? He looked around him. Obviously not. Either he was nuts, or the victim of some kind of potent witch's magic. He turned to the window again, fully expecting the witch to be gone—but there she was, with a broomstick by her side, defying gravity, wind velocity, and the laws of space, sitting on that wing as though it were her living-room sofa.

She poked a long, bony finger first at him, then at the air vent above him and made the proper motions with her fingers to ask him to turn the tiny round wheel just over his head, the wheel marked "Cold Air." Billy started not to do it, but couldn't restrain himself. He turned the vent, felt the rush of cold air, saw the witch disappear from the wing and—with a whoosh and an "ahhhhh" and a terrible rocking of the entire cabin—reappear in the vacant seat next to him.

"Relax," Witch said reassuringly. "You're the only one who can see and hear me. Excuse me while I get this broomstick out of your way. *There!*" She sighed, then wiggled her neck a bit until it popped. "I'm getting too old for air spouts, even when they are open. Oh, I could still make it through a closed vent if I had to, but at my age one prefers ducts and transoms."

"The broom . . .?" Billy whispered. "How did you get the broom down there, too?"

Witch frowned and gave him a little-boy-asking-dumb-questions look. "Hasn't anyone ever told you that witches can do *anything?*" Then, in a friendlier voice, she said, "Halloween's harder on a witch than Christmas is on Santa Claus. When I thought of that whole evening of trick-or-trick ahead of me, I just had to grab the first plane I saw and rest my feet."

Billy hesitated to correct her, but said politely, "You mean trick-or-*treat.*"

"I mean what I say!" Witch shouted, and her eyes glowed like Fourth-of-July sparklers. "Who treats a *witch?* Nope. Trick-or-*trick!*" She saw the stewardess wheeling the refreshments cart down the aisle and said, "Oh, I would dearly love a cup of tea!"

When the cart stopped by Billy's seat, he marveled at all the things on it, in it, under it. Ice buckets and snacks and carbonated drink bottles on top, napkins and glasses and openers on the middle shelves, and hundreds of tiny bottles rattling against each other near the floor. Of course, the bottles were strictly for grownups, but that didn't stop Billy from looking at them.

"And what'll you have, Billy?" the stewardess asked in a friendly voice.

"May I have a . . . cup of tea, please?" Billy asked while Witch nodded.

"Tea?" The stewardess had expected him to ask for a soft drink. Ten-year-old boys didn't usually request tea. She smiled. "There's some water boiling. It won't take a minute." She turned her back on the cart and returned to the galley.

Witch, who had been sitting quietly and invisibly, took this opportunity to reach onto the cart and grab two bottles marked G-i-n, two marked B-r-a-n-d-y, two marked V-o-d-k-a, and two marked M-a-r-t-i-n-i. She hid them in one of her deep pockets, and when she read Billy's mind, she said, "Just you *dare* say something and I'll turn you into a squirrel with a bushy tail! I'm old enough to be your great-great-great-great-great-great-grandmother and certainly I'm entitled to indulge myself when the opportunity presents itself."

Billy changed the subject. "How old *are* you?" he asked.

"That's a *very* personal question," Witch answered testily. "You mortals call yourselves curious—but you're just plain nosy. Still," she conceded, "you're nicer than most, so I'll tell you my age. I'm a nindred years old. Don't ask how old *that* is. Explaining witches' measurements is harder than explaining the new math."

The stewardess handed Billy his cup of tea on a small tray, and he thanked her for it. No sooner was her back turned than Witch commanded, "Put lemon and sugar in it!" He squeezed the wedge of lemon and added sugar. "Stir it!" she commanded again. He did so. "Hold it where I can *get* to it," she said, and when he did, she slurped it loudly and said, "That's *hot!*" Then she slurped again.

When the stewardess noticed Billy's almost empty cup she said, "You must have been thirsty. Let me know when you want some more." Billy nodded, waited until she was out of earshot, and said to Witch, "It isn't polite to slurp like that."

"May not be polite but it certainly is comforting," Witch answered. Then she reached into her pocket, pulled out the two bottles marked G-i-n, unscrewed their caps, and poured them into the teacup. She took a gulp, made a face, then said belligerently, "It is *not!*"

"I didn't say anything," Billy fenced.

"But you *thought* something. I hear thoughts as easily as I hear words. Want me to tell you what you thought?"

"What?" Billy asked cautiously.

"You thought that it's wrong to drink the contents of these bottles. It's wrong for *you* to drink, and it's wrong for teen-agers to drink. It's even wrong for grownups to drink because drinking makes them repulsive. But this stuff doesn't affect witches the way it does people. Witches are *born* repulsive. We can't help it. We just are. Besides, we're used to it. We call it witches' brew. Surely you've heard of witches' brew?"

Billy nodded. He began to feel more and more at ease with Witch as he leaned his head back against his seat and listened to her ramble on about all sorts of subjects: short skirts ("A disgrace!"), dieting (Ridiculous! I eat all I want and never gain a pound. Of course, I *exercise* a lot!"), motorcars ("I wouldn't be caught *alive* fighting the traffic on a public highway!"), and vacuum cleaners ("I'll take an old-fashioned broom any day!").

Then she opened the two bottles marked B-r-a-n-d-y, poured their contents into her teacup, deposited the empties in the large pouch in the rear of the seat in front of her (the one with the sick-sacks in it), and demanded some peanuts.

"Peanuts?" Billy asked. "Now *where*—"

"Observe, man, observe!" Witch admonished. "Don't just *look*, *observe!* There's a bowl of salted peanuts on the refreshment cart on the second shelf, just behind the napkins. Walk down the aisle yonder and get me a handful of them. Scoop up plenty of salt, too. Witches crave salt. We sweat a lot, y'know."

Billy requested the peanuts, received a paper cup filled with them, checked the salt, and returned to his seat. He caught Witch hiding the two empty V-o-d-k-a bottles in the pouch, and detected a distinct hand-in-the-cookie-jar look on her face at being caught. She pounced on the peanuts the way a cat pounces on catnip. In no time at all they were gone, right down to the last peanut skin and the last grain of salt (which stuck to her cheek).

Billy walked to the cart again and refilled the cup with peanuts. The stewardess gave him a startled look this time, but he said calmly, "I really love salted peanuts. I sweat a lot, y'know!" He carefully pinched the top of the cup so the peanuts wouldn't spill out, then propped it into the pouch where the empties were. "They're for you to take with you," he said to Witch.

"If ever I liked a mortal, I'd like you," Witch said impulsively. Then, to change the mood, "We're approaching Chicago. Got to clear out. Prefer to do my own landings."

Billy sensed a change in her—an unbecoming change. He'd heard that witches fib a lot and she'd fibbed to him about witches' brew. That stuff in the bottles was just as bad for witches as it was for everyone else. He considered telling her so, but when he remembered that witches read thoughts, he stopped thinking it.

She *was* acting odd. Her movements were jerkier and her words stuck to each other and her eyes simply would not focus. When she fished out one of the bottles marked M-a-r-t-i-n-i and started to unscrew its cap, Billy said politely, "Don't you think you've had enough?" He proceeded to enumerate the empties. "There's only one bottle left. Give it to me—and I promise you it will never be opened. Please."

"I will . . . *not!*" Witch was unconvincingly indignant. "Call it those fancy names if you want to. *I* call it *witches' brew!*" She poured the contents of the already-opened bottle into her cup, spilled a good bit of it on her dusty black skirt, dribbled some of it down her chin as she drank it, then acted as repulsive as a mortal as she barked, "Mind your own business!" Billy noticed, however, that she left the last bottle in her pocket, unopened, which was at least a slight victory. As long as she didn't open that last one, there was hope. *Poor dear*, he thought. *She needs a clear head tonight and she's all muddled*. Of course she heard him think it and replied hotly, "I am *not* muddled. Me ear is clean . . . I mean, my hell is cleared . . . I mean *my head is clear*." Then, just for good measure, she added, "*Shut up!*"

The "Fasten Your Seat Belt" light went on, and Witch pointed to the air vent. She wouldn't *ask* him to open it because she was still pouting. He did so as she reached under the seat and grasped her broom. Then he watched her point the broom handle straight at the vent, mumble something under her breath, and begin to dissolve. The plane rocked wildly as though it were encountering a series of air pockets, and Witch went out the same way she had come in.

Billy felt letdown that Witch didn't even say good-bye, but he'd learned for sure that witches aren't like people and can't be blamed for behaving differently. He turned off the air vent and glanced outside, expecting to see Witch flying away through the clouds. Instead, he almost jumped out of his skin to find her face pressed against the glass, scowling at him. The wart on the tip of her nose was barely the thickness of glass away from him. He read her lips. "Open the vent, stupid!" she said. He did as he was told, and the plane began to rock again as Witch whooshed down, grabbed the paper cup full of peanuts she'd forgotten, and whooshed out again.

"Don't be alarmed!" the pilot said over the loudspeaker in an effort to calm his passengers. "The present turbulence is due to obviated air pockets from the isolated mimjims bordering on our abdicated landing pattern."

Billy looked out, saw Witch tip the paper cup all the way up as she drained it of its last peanut, then wipe her mouth with the back of her hand. He had to say one last thing to her before she disappeared, so he closed his eyes and thought it. *"Promise* me that you'll never open that last bottle. *Please. Please."* He couldn't be sure she had heard him because all she did was wink deliciously and swoop away.

Immediately, it was calm again. The clouds had disappeared, and there was the airport below them. In three minutes they were safely on the ground, and he was walking out of the plane into his parents' arms.

It took some fast talking to get Billy's mother to agree to his trick-or-treating. "I don't like the way you look," she kept saying. "I can't put my finger on it, but you seem flushed. Have you a stomach ache?"

Billy shook his head. "I feel fine. The plane ride was kinda bumpy, that's all."

"Well, thirty minutes—and not a minute more! It would be a shame not to let you wear this wonderful mask I bought you."

Billy *did* flush then. His mother handed him a mask that covered his eyes and nose. The nose on the mask was long and humped and angled on its end. And right on the very tip was a wart, exactly the size of the one. . . .

"Throw this old black cape around you, Billy. And here's a brand new broom to ride on. People won't have to figure out what you're supposed to be. You're a witch!"

When he put on the cape and adjusted the mask, she shivered. "And a scary one!"

As he straddled his broom down the sidewalk, he was conscious of the wind catching up piles of dead leaves and transforming them into miniature funnels before gusting them away. The trees slapped their branches against street lights. The houses on both sides of the street had their porch lights on, and people were primed to answer doorbells the minute they rang.

"Ooooh, I'm *frightened!*" one lady said mockingly as she saw Billy. Then she looked closely at that awful nose with the rubbery wart on it and took a couple of steps backward. "You look too *real*," she whispered oddly, proffering her tray of treats but holding back as far as she could. Billy took one apple, one popcorn ball, three small candy bars, some jelly beans, and some candy corn. Into his sack they went, and after saying, "Thank you" quickly, he ran to the next porch.

Time flew by and soon there were only five minutes left of his promised thirty. His bag of treats was almost full. He should have called it quits and returned home, but one more house at the far end of the street beckoned to him. It was dark and spooky-looking and it seemed to be pulling him toward it.

He paused before the pitch-black front porch. A piece of loose siding that had been slapping in the wind suddenly began to beat its brains out against the side of the house. Leaves had blown themselves into thick piles in the corners of the porch and their rustling in the dark made him wonder if some sort of animal might not be crouching under them.

He stepped onto the porch, started to turn and run, but forced himself to advance to the doorbell and ring it. There was no answer. He rang it again. People who left their houses on Halloween night were asking to be tricked. Sometimes kids threw rocks and gravel onto their porches or littered a place with toilet paper. Billy wouldn't stoop that low. Wearing a mask didn't give you the right to act like a hoodlum.

No sooner had he turned his back to leave than the front door opened and a small woman in a white robe appeared. "We thought you youngsters had called it a night," she said pleasantly. "There were many more than we counted on, and we've nothing left to treat with except . . . these. Take them all." She put on the porch light, opened the screen door, and handed Billy four cellophane sacks filled with salted peanuts.

Billy started to tell her what an appropriate gift peanuts were for a witch, but he just took them, thanked her, and started home.

As he reached the corner of his own block, the wind grew suddenly fierce. It looked and sounded exactly like an airplane speeding up its motors before a takeoff. The wind kicked up dust the same way. Billy threw himself against the wind, but he found that he dropped back two yards for every yard he advanced.

"Give up?"

The voice sounded familiar. He peeked over his shoulder and saw another mask identical to his own—except the mask he saw wasn't a mask at all. It was Witch herself, her peaked hat pulled down tightly onto her forehead, her black cape billowing straight out, neck high.

"Hey, cut it out!" Billy pleaded. "Calm this wind!"

It stopped so suddenly that he fell down. One minute he was leaning against the wind with all his might. The next he was rolling over and over in a pile of leaves. Fortunately, his bag of treats was still intact where he had dropped it.

"Oh, dear!" Witch said. "I didn't mean to knock you off your feet. I had to find you and apologize. You were so thoughtful—and I didn't even say good-bye."

Billy was touched. "Aw, that's all right."

"No it isn't. Witches aren't used to kindness. That's why we're so nasty. If I were around you very long, I'd turn into something sweet and lovable—and who *ever* heard of a sweet and lovable witch? Why, the other witches would take away all my privileges!" She lowered her voice. "Didn't happen to trick any peanuts, did you?"

Billy suspected that she already knew the answer, but he went along with her. "Why, yes—the lady in the big house gave me all she had left."

He handed Witch three of the bags. "I've really got to go home now," he said and started toward his own house.

Witch tore open the bags and started popping handfuls of peanuts into her mouth as she walked side-by-side with Billy down the quiet, shadowy street. Neither said a word until they were standing at the gate to Billy's yard.

"I like you," she said. "I like you very much." Then, confidentially, "If ever you get in a jam and need a witch to nullify a spell or undo a hex, just think of me and I'll come flying. If I wasn't so fond of you, I'd steal that brand new broom. I've ridden this old broom of mine until it's a disgrace."

"Take it," Billy insisted without hesitation. "And take the last bag of peanuts, too. I'm sorry I held out on you."

Witch looked as though she were going to cry. She'd known, of course. If he held out on her—why, she had the right to hold out on him. But now—

"What can I give you?" she asked. "What would you like? Name anything."

"Nothing for me," Billy said. "But I do want something."

"Name it. Just name it."

"I want you to promise me that you will never drink another drop of that . . . witches' brew. It makes you act . . . well, *silly*. I was proud of you today when you didn't open that last bottle. If you never open it—or another like it—that will be my present."

Witch made a small choking sound. It didn't sound like anything Billy had ever heard before. Using the hem of her cape to dap her eyes, she said softly, "Imagine that! Proud of *me*! *You* were proud of *me*!" Quickly she traded brooms. Looking straight at Billy she said, "It's the first time I've cried in a nindred years!" Then she smiled thinly, clutched her peanuts, turned, and flew away, trailing what seemed to be a million crackly leaves behind her.

Before he could stretch his feet all the way down between the cool, clean sheets of his own bed, Billy was sound asleep. Billy's father came in to say good night, found his son asleep, tucked him in, and then joined Billy's mother in the living room.

"It's good to have him home again," she said. "He was

gone just a few days, yet he seems somehow to have grown up. He's more sure of himself."

Billy's father smiled. "Maybe he's sure of himself when he's awake, but he's the same little boy he always was when he's asleep."

Billy's father walked over to his wife's chair. "I want to show you something very interesting. I found it under Billy's pillow. *This*."

He opened his hand and revealed a small bottle, capped and sealed. It was labeled M-a-r-t-i-n-i. "He must have taken it for a souvenir of his flight. I found it quite by accident when I lifted his pillow to straighten it. I'll slip it back in place so it'll be there in the morning. He'll bring it down to breakfast and show it to us then . . . And guess what else was there? Three salted peanuts —squashed."

"Oh, dear." Billy's mother sighed. "He never was one to put things under his pillow." She looked puzzled. "I'll never know what happened to my brand new broom. When I asked him how he lost it, he said he'd explain someday—and I'm sure he will. He had a strange look in his eyes when he talked about the broom. A . . . soft look. If it were anything except a broom, I'd suspect him of giving it to someone he had fallen in love with."

A sudden sharp burst of wind made the windows rattle and the back door bang and a strange commotion come and go in the fireplace chimney.

Both parents were quiet for awhile, then they turned off the lights and climbed the stairs. Billy's father stood at the door of Billy's room, studied his sleeping son, replaced the bottle under the boy's pillow, and then walked slowly down the hall. He started to undress, yawned, thought of something, then said, partly to his wife and partly to himself, "Salted peanuts! I had no idea he was so fond of salted peanuts!"

The Passionate Groundhog

The Passionate Groundhog

Before sharing this story about a passionate groundhog named Jerry, you must understand that people behavior resembles groundhog behavior. There are boy groundhogs and girl groundhogs who have happy love affairs and unhappy love affairs, punctuated with heart throbs and heartaches. Understand, too, that groundhogs, alas (like people, alas), sometimes get themselves into sticky situations and devilish messes. So if Jerry Groundhog finds himself in a compromising position because of his love for Geraldine, be generous and forgive him. People are only human. Jerry is only groundhog.

Once upon a time there lived in a hole in the ground a handsome bachelor groundhog named Jerry. Jerry's coat was a deep, rich brown, and he brushed and brushed it until it had a sleek and irridescent shine. He was privately proud of the way his ears lay back neatly against his head.

(Groundhogs are by nature emotional and when they are agitated their ears stand up straight and begin to flutter.) Jerry's nails were impeccably clean, his figure trim and supple. He chewed grass shoots every day to keep his breath sweet and inoffensive. Anyway you looked at it, he was a first-class, top-drawer groundhog.

And no wonder! Jerry was the grandson of the grandson of the grandson of the original founder of Groundhog Day. He was, by inheritance and succession, the undisputed champion weather predictor of the whole wide world. Crowds of shivering people waited patiently outside his burrow each February second (and millions more turned on their TV sets) to observe Jerry as he emerged from his long confinement underground. If the sun was shining and he saw his shadow, he promptly returned to his quarters, leaving the world to worry with six more weeks of winter. However, if the day was gloomy enough so that shadows didn't show, he officially announced the arrival of spring six weeks early. Jerry's word was law. If he saw his shadow, people went out and bought shovels and snow tires and kept on shivering. If he didn't see it, people felt a sudden warmth, salted away their woolies in mothballs, and bought tulip bulbs in assorted colors for immediate planting.

Every year, long before Thanksgiving, on the day the first leaf fell from the first tree, Jerry began his search for suitable winter quarters. It was as much a chore as looking for a people-apartment can be. The dirt had to be of a firm consistency, yet porous enough for a groundhog to breathe through. Rocks could be a nuisance, especially if they hampered you from burrowing down a respectable distance. (You don't have to be a groundhog to know that the deeper you dig, the warmer you are when the surface crusts with snow and ice.)

He settled finally for a spot not far from a modest-sized stream that wound its way to a cliff, where it actually turned into a tiny waterfall. Here he began to dig, first straight down, then obliquely, tunnel-wise, until he had hollowed out a snug living room, bedroom, and kitchen. (Who needs a dining room when nobody comes for dinner?)

You've heard that groundhogs detest bright sunlight, but did you know that total darkness bothers them almost as much? So for centuries intelligent groundhogs, like Jerry, have traded warmth and food to fireflies in exchange for light in their underground homes. Jerry invited the same firefly family each year because he found them compatible. They slept when he slept and they kept a discreet distance.

As soon as he'd scooped out his last pawful of dirt, stored his goodly supply of nuts, roots, and herbs in a corner of the kitchen, and installed his fireflies, Jerry carefully plastered himself into his winter home by sealing the aboveground opening to his tunnel. He did this with layer after layer of mud, which he knew would harden enough to withstand the weight of a fox or dog or even the step of a hunter who might tread unknowingly on Jerry's roof. Then he sealed the underground end of the tunnel, and as soon as he had done so, he stepped back, admired his snug, draft-free quarters, and scratched a thin line on the kitchen wall to denote the first day of his hibernation. It was November thirteenth, and there'd be a scratch per day until February second. (He didn't really need this homemade calendar because his age-old instinct always told him when the proper day arrived, but it was nice to have a double check.) Jerry was pleased with his work, and as he closed his eyes for his first nap in the new home, he said aloud to himself, "I am a self-sufficient, contented groundhog. There's nothing else in the world I could possibly want. Nothing at all."

Pay no attention to people who tell you that ground-hogs are completely dormant during their winter seclusion. Not true. Jerry's behavior was typical. While he slept a lot to make the time move faster, he was far too restless to conk out for the whole three months. He continued to brush his coat and do his nails regularly, and he kept his figure trim by moving briskly once a day from bedroom to living room to kitchen, and then just as briskly back from kitchen to living room to bedroom. As it turned out, it was this jogging routine which precipitated the terrible crisis in his life. Had he stayed put, had he curled up and slept his time out, he would never have heard the humming, he would never have known Geraldine, he would never have traded his contentment for misery and frustration. Worst of all, had an immobile Jerry slept the whole winter away there'd be no more to this story, and wouldn't *that* be ridiculous?

He was on one of his daily constitutionals when he first heard the sound through the living-room wall. Of course he didn't believe it, so he kept right on moving. But when he returned to the precise spot and heard the humming again, he stopped and listened. Groundhog ears are marvelously attuned to sounds, and it didn't take long to place the humming at three inches of dirt away from his living-room wall. There was another, a stranger sound accompanying the humming, but Jerry wasn't sure what that could be.

He was both curious and excited and he rubbed his head hard against the wall to hear more plainly. A few grains of dirt came loose and tickled his ear, causing him to pull away, scratch the tickle, then listen again.

It was most definitely a humming, and a feminine voice was doing it. If you've ever hummed with your mouth open, you know exactly what it sounded like. It couldn't be called singing. It was more of a crooning without words.

Jerry pressed his head harder against the dirt wall, held his breath, then jumped from surprise when he heard a voice say distinctly, "Geraldine, I do wish you'd stop that singing or humming or whatever it is you do. It makes me nervous."

"But, Mother," a younger voice answered, "I only hum when I brush my coat." (*That* was the other sound—*brushing!*) "It only lasts for a hundred brushstrokes, morning and night. Can't you stand it that long? Oh, dear, now I've lost count."

"I guess so," the older voice answered agreeably. "Forgive my sounding like a grouchhog. There's no harm in humming—I guess—especially when you brush by it. There's never been a groundhog who got so many compliments on the glossiness and beauty of her coat. It makes a mother proud as a person when she hears others call her daughter a raving beauty."

An indefinable, new feeling came over Jerry, a feeling he had never experienced before. It wasn't unpleasant, but it wasn't altogether pleasant, either. When he tried to analyze it, he was able to distinguish among its components such things as yearning, tenderness, aloneness —and a longing for something he had never known before. He gave himself a hard shake to get rid of it, but it stubbornly persisted. What did it mean? Was he running a fever? He felt his nose to see if it was hot. His nose was nice and cool. *What did it mean?* Up to this very moment he had always considered himself self-sufficient. Whenever friends twitted him on his bachelordom, he accused them of being envious of his freedom and charged their remarks to sour grapes. Independence had been his watchword, and now, all of a sudden, he didn't *like* being independent. He was uptight—and he was lonely. He wanted desperately to meet the raving beauty on the other side of the wall. Could it be that he was in love with her? Surely not. He'd never been in love. Besides, how could he be in love with a groundhog he'd never laid his eyes on? But he was on fire. Her voice, her humming, her mother's description of her glossiness —those things all seemed to combine to make him burn. He pressed his head so hard against the wall it hurt his whole face, but he didn't care. He mustn't miss a note of the humming which had started again, although on a softer level. And now, by concentrating with all his might, he could actually hear the brushing, too. He began to count with her: One . . . two . . . three . . . four . . . The sound of her brushing was too much for him to bear. He backed away shakily and moved into the kitchen, where he had to lean against the wall for support.

For the next two days he scarcely moved from his listening post. His face was scratched and his ears sore from where he'd pressed hard and long against the dirt wall, but he no longer cared about his appearance. He had changed in forty-eight hours from a vain, self-satisfied male concerned solely with creature comforts to a miserable, lovesick groundhog who wanted something out of his reach. His appetite dwindled; his temper flared. He was ashamed of himself for taking out his frustrations on the helpless fireflies who lived with him. He'd shout at them for making too much light (or too little) even though it wasn't their fault. His revised waking-sleeping routine confused them. The fireflies, unused to lovesick landlords, became erratic; one moment, their light would be too bright, the next it would waver and be too dim, and then it would fade away entirely.

It was Geraldine who rapped first. She, too, had heard a voice—a male voice—first scolding, then apologizing to the fireflies. She listened for the sound of a female voice, and when none came through, she knew that her feminine instinct was right in assuring her that the shouter in the adjoining apartment was a bachelor. The same instinct told her that she herself would be somehow involved with the attractive-sounding male who was so near and yet so far. She sensed the inner feelings behind the sound of his voice. Was it possible for a hemmed-in bachelor's frustration waves to travel through three inches of dirt and find an understanding head and heart on the other side? Why not? It had happened in the people world. A high wall could not separate Romeo from Juliet. Why should a few inches of earth separate Jerry from Geraldine?

Her taps were timid at first, but when they were answered with fervent taps from his side, she tapped harder. Before she realized it, the taps had changed to raps.

Finally she yelled at him, "Say something!"

"I love you!" he yelled back, surprising himself as much as he did Geraldine with the words he'd never in his whole life said before.

"But you haven't even seen me!"

"I love you anyway."

She wanted to ask him a dozen questions. Was he dark brown or light tan? Were his eyes black or amber? Had he ever been in love before? But all she could manage was, "What's your name?"

"Jerry!"

"I'm Geraldine."

"I know."

"I live with my mother."

"I know."

"She's nervous—and she's *very* strict."

"Oh." Then Jerry added (very softly, under his breath, because it was a naughty word), "Hell."

"I can't hear you."

"Is she well?"

"Oh, she's well. But not well enough to learn about you. So let me rap first. When I rap, you'll know it's safe to talk. OK?"

"Yes." And then, very softly again, he said another naughty word which expressed his feelings at having to wait to talk to his beloved. "Damn."

"Speak louder."

"Yes, ma'am."

And that's the way it worked out. As soon as Geraldine's mother was asleep, Geraldine ran to the partition that separated the lovers and gave several quick raps. Jerry, who spent most of his time waiting on his side of the partition, gave his answering raps, and their conversations would begin.

What did they talk about? The usual things. Their likes and dislikes (both adored hickory nuts and hated acorns), their views on marriage (once is for always), child-rearing (love with discipline), Jerry's illustrious ancestors, Geraldine's mother's nerves—subjects such as that.

And then, on a day in mid-December, they talked too long. Geraldine blamed herself for it. She had expected her mother to awaken at any time, but Jerry was so happy talking to her she couldn't bear to make him stop.

"I cannot stand this separation any longer," he said, his voice aimed in Geraldine's direction, his nose directly against the dirt. "I'm going to dig a hole in the wall so we can see each other and talk easier."

Geraldine didn't answer. She had seen her mother slouched by the doorway, listening to every word Jerry was saying. Her mother's light tan coat had taken on a greenish hue and her ears were fluttering wildly.

"Did you hear me, honey?" Jerry repeated in a burst of passion. "I'm coming through."

Geraldine's mother sprang to the spot where his announcement had come from and screamed at the wall, "Oh, no, you're not!"

Silence.

Jerry guessed what had happened. And then he heard Geraldine whine, "Now, Mother—"

"Don't you 'Now, Mother' me you . . . you . . . flirt! So he wants to come through, does he? I should say not! Next thing we know he'll be calling me Mother! No, no, no, no! It wouldn't be proper. Not underground!" And then she made her point, most dramatically, by fainting.

Silence again. Jerry stayed frozen to the spot, his nose still against the wall, too shocked, too stunned to move.

Geraldine worked frantically—slapping her mother's cheeks, rubbing her paws, and finally bringing her around, only to hear her mother gasp, "Not proper at all!" before fainting again.

When she was revived for keeps, Geraldine's mother said, "We'll continue this conversation where we can enjoy privacy."

Slowly, Jerry pulled his nose away from the wall and slumped to the floor. The fireflies—the very ones he had yelled at—felt so sorry for him in his dejection that they put on their super-brights to cheer him up. Poor Geraldine, he thought. His heart ached for her and the bad time he knew she was having while he was unable to be of any help. It was an entirely new experience for him. Never before had he worried about any one other than himself.

"Who is he?" Geraldine's mother asked sternly, once she was certain no one could hear. "Who is he?"

"His name is Jerry and he's adorable and I love him."

"*Love* him? You haven't even *seen* him! For all we know he's an amorous aardvark out for a fling, or some willy-nilly woodchuck with questionable intentions!" (In moments of stress groundhogs often refer to other groundhogs as aardvarks or woodchucks.)

"He speaks highly of his family," Geraldine said. "From the way he talks, he's some kind of groundhog royalty."

"Royalty?"

"Yes, and y'know what? I really and truly think he's telling the truth."

Geraldine's mother seemed to relax the tiniest bit. "If that's so . . . It seems preposterous on the face of it, but if it's so. . . ."

"Oh, Mother! *Mother!*" Geraldine pleaded. "Please, please *find out!*"

"I will," her mother promised in a composed voice. Her ears lay flat as she said it, her coat was its normal tan again. "I may have to surface to do it, but I'll find out!"

For three days there was no tapping. Jerry scarcely budged from the partition through which Geraldine had talked with him. He took the briefest of cat naps for fear of missing a message from her. He could only guess that Geraldine had sworn not to communicate with him. He hoped and prayed it was nothing worse than that. Once he even threw caution to the winds and rapped without her rapping first. There was no answer. He had no way of knowing that Geraldine was alone, miserably alone, on her side of the partition while her mother was above-ground doing her investigation. When he heard no raps, no sounds at all, he wondered (although it broke his heart to do so) if Geraldine's mother had actually taken Geraldine away, perhaps forever.

It was equally hard for Geraldine to look at the familiar wall through which had come so much happiness and not be able to reassure Jerry that she was all right. But a promise was a promise, and she knew what her mother's first question would be the minute she returned.

"You *didn't*—?" her mother asked, as they were re-mudding the tunnel entrance which they had opened for her mother's surfacing.

"I didn't."

"I'm proud of you, my *dear*." There was something reassuring about the way her mother pronounced the words "my *dear*."

"Well?" Geraldine was bursting with questions, but she could manage just that one word.

"I was discreet, naturally. But I was thorough. I found many mutual friends. What Jerry told you is true. If anything, he was too modest. He is *the* Groundhog Day groundhog.

"No!"

"Yes. And he's dutiful, respectful of his elders, a hard worker, and from what I've learned, I feel he'll be a good provider."

"Then . . ." Now it was Geraldine whose ears were fluttering. "Then you approve?"

"My *dear*," Geraldine's mother answered in that same prim voice she had used earlier, "*I approve*." The way she said those two words said it all. They said: *a good*

groundhog-bachelor (like a good people-bachelor) is hard to
find and when you meet a catch, catch him.

Geraldine ached to run to the wall to tell Jerry the
happy news, but her mother continued speaking in that
same calm, relaxed voice. "When spring comes and we
leave our underground homes for the top of the earth,
you two will be married. There'll be blue and yellow
flowers—dandelions and clover—raindrop punch . . .
corn cookies . . . Cousin Ginny will croon *'Because'* . . .
and, oh, it will be nice . . . *nice.*" Her voice trailed away
dreamily.

"Mother," Geraldine ventured. "The . . . *tunnel?*"

"Still not proper." The answer was immediate and
final, but even so, it was an automatic response.
Geraldine's mother was busy visualizing more important
things than tunnels. There would be showers for the
bride, parties for the two families, a wedding breakfast
with plenty of sassafras roots, and. . . .

"Just a *tiny* tunnel?"

"No." Firmly, irrevocably. The subject was closed.

So Jerry and Geraldine became engaged, and they
nestled their noses into the wall of dirt that separated
them and acted exactly like lovesick creatures have acted
since the beginning of time. Each sighed into the other's
almost-nose, each whispered sweet nothings into the
other's almost-ear, and each waited, but not patiently, for
spring.

It was Geraldine who first brought up the subject of
Jerry's shadow. "Darling," she ventured. "Mother says we

can get married when spring comes, but . . . *what if you see your shadow?* You are the one who announces spring's official arrival. What if the sun is shining when you emerge? Oh, Jerry! You wouldn't make the two of us suffer this way six weeks longer than necessary . . . *would you?*"

There was a long silence while Jerry thought of his great heritage, of his responsibility to the world, of the honor involved in his tradition. Then he thought of his burning passion—and how he just couldn't stand it if he had to suffer three whole inches of dirt away from his beloved Geraldine six weeks longer! But if the sun was shining, he couldn't help but see his shadow, could he? And if he saw his shadow, he'd have to come back into this lonely apartment for six torturous weeks, wouldn't he? Why, Geraldine might get so provoked at him she wouldn't even whisper through the wall! *Oh me, oh my*, he thought. *Was ever a groundhog faced with a greater problem since the world began?*

January came and went. Thirty-one scratches on the kitchen-wall calendar. One more scratch and February first was gone. Tomorrow would be the day! Worry made Jerry pale. He neglected the nails on his paws, and his ears, instead of lying back neatly the way they had been trained, behaved in a crazy way: one stood up, the other drooped. It wasn't that Jerry didn't *care* any more. He was so busy wrestling with his conscience he had no time to think of his appearance.

And then it was February second. Wearily, after a night

without sleep, Jerry started to unseal the tunnel entrance and aim for daylight. He paused long enough for one last look behind him, and at that precise moment, without any warning that it would happen, he saw the dirt partition begin to crumble. And all of a sudden there were Geraldine's precious paws poking through the partition. The paws were holding something—waving it wildly so he'd be sure to see it. Geraldine's voice came through crystal clear. "Quick, Jerry! Put these on before you leave. I made them myself from dried leaves."

Sunglasses.

Sunglasses!

"I used bark for the rims and I didn't have any glue so I—I spit on them. Wear them and you won't be able to *see* if the sun is out!"

"Huh?"

"You won't be able to see your shadow even if there *is* a shadow!"

Jerry took the glassless glasses, but before putting them on, he peeked through the hole and saw Geraldine. He knew immediately what he had suspected all along: she was the most beautiful creature he had ever laid eyes on. Her face! Those pointed ears! Such delicate hairs in the nostrils! Such sharp, even teeth! *Gorgeous!*

When he stuck his snout through the hole in the wall to give Geraldine a kiss, he got such a stiff push in the face from Geraldine's side that he went reeling backward. He picked himself up, looked through the hole to learn what had prompted the push, and saw Geraldine being jerked to the other side of the room by her mother, who kept mumbling, "It isn't proper. It isn't proper. It isn't proper." Then she fainted all over again.

Jerry, wearing Geraldine's homemade sunglasses, clambered out of his tunnel and pranced about on the outside just as his great-great-great-great-grandfather had done. No one in the crowd of onlookers, including press, radio, and television people, noticed that his ears were fluttering as they had never fluttered before as he issued his statement: "I, Jerry Groundhog, do hereby declare that I *cannot* see my shadow. Hence, spring will be six weeks *early* this year!" Then, because he couldn't see what he was doing, as he took a step backward, he lost his footing, landed smack in the tunnel opening, and fell all the way down the hole he'd just emerged from. But he didn't mind the bruises. Once below ground, he threw off the glasses, went boldly to the hole in the wall, and yelled, "Come on out, Mother! Spring is here!"

To this day Jerry doesn't know whether the sun actually did shine on that particular February second. He had said he could not see his shadow and he had told the truth. He couldn't see anything! Years later, whenever he told the story to his own sons—and then to his own grandsons —he even added his own moral: If you don't *look* for trouble, you won't *find* it!

On February fourteenth, Valentine's Day, Jerry and Geraldine were married near the little waterfall. Yes, and there were blue and yellow flowers—dandelions and clover—raindrop punch . . . corn cookies . . . Cousin Ginny sang 'Because' . . . and, oh, it was nice . . . *nice.*

The Red-Haired Leprechaun

The Red-Haired Leprechaun

Notice: If you do not believe in leprechauns, stop before you begin. Save your eyes. And save the pride of any leprechaun who might be nearby. It's a hard slap to be read about and not believed in!

Leprechauns exist.

Anyone who has seen these little fellows (small in size but great in powers) can tell you they are thick as flies along the Sea of Moyle, inside caves and under waterfalls in the County of Connacht, and in splendid supply in the regions ruled by Tara the King.

Moyle, Connacht, Tara—unaccustomed-sounding names and not the kind you'll find on an Irish road map (as you would Limerick, for instance, or Killarney, or Cork), but there's a reason for that, too. Leprechauns prefer to use the place names their kinsmen have used since (and we might as well begin at the beginning) forever.

Question a certain barber in Ballinaboy and he'll tell you he's well acquainted with a specific leprechaun, Larry by name. Sees him maybe once a month, orders shoes from him, fishes with him occasionally (on opposite banks; leprechauns feel safer when humans keep their distance), loves him as a brother.

The Larry of our story lives in the hollow behind the ruins of an ancient castle on the north shore of Lake Corrib. It might be Castlekirke—*might* be, mind you —and then again it might not. Find yourself a piece of old ruin and you won't have to search for leprechauns. But if you're like most people, you'll walk right by them because of their green clothes (the exact color and shade of grass). Larry finds lakeside living convenient, especially for washing socks and underwear. On moonless nights he sometimes strips and lets the mist above the waters steam out wrinkles from his green outer garments. Not often, though, because the dampness riles his rheumatism. Alas, rheumatic aches and pains are endured from one end of the Emerald Isle to the other by mortals and leprechauns alike.

Larry's troubles began on the thirteenth day of the thirteenth month, a traditional time for leprechauns in the Tara area to congregate for their annual meeting. The thirteenth month was a hectic one, anyway, because it was added to the calendar for the doing of things left undone the rest of the year. Never keen on these yearly conclaves, Larry was less inclined than ever to attend this

year's meeting. His friend Brendan had paid him a special
visit just to scold him for missing last year's council and to
make him promise that he would not miss this year's.
Having given his word, there was nothing to do but go
—even though a voice inside himself kept saying, "Don't
go, don't go."

"Fellow Lurikeens—"
Danny-the-Leader used the traditional salutation as he
commenced addressing what surely was no more than a
bank of waving grass and leaves. But Danny's trained eyes
saw his audience clearly. There were at least twenty small
ones scattered about. Some were in treetops, others
under bracken and golden gorse. Each had a gray, puck-
ered face under a green, pointed hat; each owned a
knobby nose and bushy eyebrows; and almost all had thin
fringes of gray whiskers sprouting downward from their
chins.

"I don't like these get-togethers any more than you do,"
Danny said honestly, "but it was decreed by the Sons of
the Rock four thousand years ago that certain fairies,
banshees, and we who are sometimes called lurikeens
should meet once a year for the gathering together of
loose ends, as it were."

He paused while he stared at Patrick, an older leprechaun who was seated on a moss-covered rock near a
tree stump. Patrick was scratching himself vigorously—as
he always did, year in and year out. Danny-the-Leader
found it difficult to think on his feet while a front-row
spectator was scratching away like a monkey.

"Pat-*rick*—" he began, his voice going up on the "rick" in a warning way. "Still at it?" There were times when Danny was sure that Patrick's scratching was no more than an attention-getting device. Even though leprechauns have tender skins, they seldom if ever itch.

Sure enough, as soon as he was singled out, Patrick stopped.

"That's better!" Danny said approvingly, then quickly changed the subject. "Our first bit of business is a complaint registered against Tommy." He looked for Tommy but couldn't find him. "Tommy! Where are you, Tommy?" He asked the question impatiently. Tommy was the youngest of the leprechauns and he shouldn't be clever enough to elude the leader's searching eyes.

"Here," squeaked Tommy from where his body was completely hidden by a fuchsia hedge. The green of his hat blended so perfectly into the leaves of the shrub that only his blue eyes were distinguishable. Then, before Danny could begin his lacing, Tommy whined, "Are you going to pick on me *again*? Every year—"

Danny interrupted him. "Every year the complaints get louder." Then, sarcastically, "Sure and I'll bet you haven't the *foggiest* notion *why*?"

"I *try*. Really, sir, I *try*. I make shoes from dawn till dusk. Fairies praise the shoes I make. Humans, too. Last month I made a pair of dancing slippers for Sean O'Sullivan, and he danced all night without a bit of tiredness."

Tommy's injured innocence was too self-pitying, too pat. "It's not shoes I'm referring to, and you know it!"

Danny's voice was stern. "You work from dawn to dusk, you say. All well and good. But what do you do *after* dusk, me boy?"

Tommy fidgeted. "I do what most self-respecting leprechauns do. I go about the town and peek into windows to be certain the humans are asleep—"

The other leprechauns began to squirm uncomfortably.

"And then I slip inside the houses and find where they've hidden their money and—"

There was a murmur of protest. The others knew very well what Tommy did because each one of them did precisely the same thing—only they didn't *talk* about it. It wasn't as if they *stole* anything. Why, every Irishman knows exactly what leprechauns do after dark, but you'll never hear it mentioned. They shave the barest smidgin of gold from the flat side of every coin, collect the precious bits in a leather pouch, and when they get home, they empty their shavings into a crock of gold. Every leprechaun worth his salt owns a secret vessel and works nights filling it. The reason is plain: If ever a mortal man captures a leprechaun and holds onto him and won't let him go, the little fellow can (as a last extremity) buy his freedom with his crock of gold.

"No use repeating what is common knowledge," Danny said, interrupting Tommy's monologue. "But *you*, Tommy-O, instead of shaving off just a wee whisker here and there, you've been clipping pieces and chipping chunks off peoples' money in a most obvious way. That's greed, Tommy, greed. A crock of gold filled with greed will land you in the strong arms of a greedy mortal every time. Mend your ways."

"Yes, sir," Tommy answered, almost with relief at being lectured for doing what he knew was wrong. "I'll try. I'll really try."

"Do that," Danny-the-Leader said, sounding like a schoolteacher. Then, changing his whole mood and tone of voice, he said cheerfully, "Stand up, Brendan. Stand up and be commended."

Surprised at hearing his name, Brendan, the oldest (rumored to be at least 350) and the most wizened of the leprechauns, sat up from where he had been lying on a soft cover of heather and moss and slowly got to his feet.

"A pleasure to announce that Brendan, who can use gold as much as the next man (Danny shot a look at Tommy) has the kindest heart in Tara. For years he has refused to take so much as a thank-you for the shoes he makes for elderly fairies. I also happen to know Brendan made ten pairs of shoes for children in a tinker caravan last winter. Measured their feet while they were asleep and left the finished shoes nearby." It was an effort for Danny to control his emotions. "Most of us distrust the tinkers. We call them gypsies and shun them. Not Brendan. He saw neither tinkers nor gypsies. He saw only little children whose feet were bare and cold. Take a bow, Brendan."

The old leprechaun was as self-conscious as he was generous. He nodded shyly, then dived behind a rock where he stayed out of sight while all the others whistled and stamped their feet. (A bruised palm can interfere with the delicate profession of fairy shoemaking, so leprechauns seldom applaud with their hands.)

Danny puzzled for a moment about how he should broach the final bit of business for the day. Then, with a gesture which plainly said, "Here's the proper way!" he assumed his schoolteacher voice again and ordered, "Each of you will stand . . . and remove his hat!"

Rumblings of back talk came from some. Leprechauns dislike going bareheaded even for a moment because their heads are sensitive to drafts. Without the protection of a soft wool head covering, one can catch the nuisance of a cold.

"Stand . . . and take off your hats . . . *all* of you!" Knowing what they were thinking, Danny added, "Only for half a minute. Then you can put them on again."

Some popped up, some jumped down, and soon all were standing in something of a row, their bald heads reflecting the rays of sunshine like highly polished mirrors.

"Is everybody standing?" Danny asked. *"Everybody?"*

Slowly, slowly, Larry got to his feet.

Looking directly at Larry, Danny said, "Your hat, Larry. Hurry. Remove your hat."

When they are embarrassed, leprechauns do not blush. Instead of blushing, they stammer. "B-but, s-*sir*—" Larry managed feebly.

"Waiting," Danny said. By this time every bare head was turned toward Larry. "Your hat, *please!*"

Larry sighed, kicked himself for letting Brendan talk him into coming to the council against his own better judgment, then reluctantly removed his hat.

The communal gasp sounded like an explosion. Nor did it stay in one spot and slowly fade away. First it hit the flaky old stone wall, then it bounced off the wall and rebounded against two tall tree trunks, then it ricocheted back to the lake itself, where it sank into the water with a gurgle.

The leprechauns were totally stunned to see a thick head of flaming red hair instead of Larry's accustomed baldness.

For one paralyzed moment there was not a sound. Birds stopped singing. Patrick stopped scratching. No one seemed to breathe the tight and heavy air. Then one of the little people pointed at Larry and said loudly, "Why, he's as odd as two is even!" Someone else caught the thought and repeated it: "Larry's as odd as two is even!" Like quicksilver, the words fanned out to all corners of the assemblage. "He's as odd as two is even!" The last one to say it did so with a titter. The leprechaun standing next to him caught the titter and turned it into a giggle. Someone at the far end of the glade caught the giggle and transformed it into a snort. Then all of a sudden there was a roar of spontaneous laughter. Louder and louder the leprechauns whooped at the sight of poor Larry, looking small and foolish with his bushy head exposed.

To any self-respecting leprechaun hair is silly, and because he doesn't wear the stuff, he'll tell you that baldness earns respect and betokens wisdom. A gleaming knob makes a man look worldly, distinguished, handsome. And besides, who wants hair? *People* have hair!

Leprechauns cannot shed tears, not even tears of laughter, but several of the group did the next best thing and doubled up, rolling over and over on the green carpet, screaming with hysterics. One or two darted up to Larry and pulled at his hair to see if it was actually growing in by the roots. It was, of course, and it hurt when they did that.

"Pipe down!" Danny shouted at them. "Pipe down this minute or I'll make you pay a forfeit from your crocks of gold!" That threat never failed to have an immediate sobering effect on his audience because a leprechaun would sooner be whipped than give up the tiniest bit of dust from his treasure. The laughter died in the reverse order of its buildup—wild howls to belly laughs to snorts to giggles to titters and, finally, to silence.

"Just one question, Larry, me boy," Danny said. "In fact, just one word: *Why?*"

Larry was too miserable to invent a story or to protest his innocence, as Tommy had tried to do, so he told the truth. "I've always been bald. At least it seems like always. And I've never wanted to be any other way . . . But when the banshee gave me the present, I tried a bit of it out of curiosity and I got the hair."

"*Banshee?*" Danny spoke the word cautiously, and as he did so, an ominous uneasiness settled over the group. Banshees are fairy women who wander uphill and down dale because they have no place to live. You can always tell when they are nearby because they let out terrible wails, and each wail is an announcement that a high-born person is about to die. Some who have seen the banshees say they draw combs through their hair as they cry out. Others say, no, not combs, *fingernails*. They tear their hair as they mourn. Then they use magic to regrow it when the grief is past. Banshees know about hair.

"*Banshee?*" Danny repeated grimly, demanding an answer.

Larry nodded. The shock of being laughed at was wearing off. Now Larry was angry, angrier at the rude behavior of his peers than he was ashamed of the way he looked to them. Unlike Tommy, he had done nothing underhanded. If anything, his hair was the result of an act of kindness. The more he thought, the madder he got.

"Yes, banshee!" Larry said defiantly. "Her name was Deirdre and she had caught her leg in a hunter's trap. I opened the trap, bandaged her leg, and brought her food until she was able to walk again. She gave me the . . . the Stuff . . . for a present. It's in a bottle that never empties. Use a little or use a lot, and that much more comes to fill its place."

Brendan spoke up. "Does it really grow hair? Really and truly?"

"Really and truly!" Larry answered, standing a little taller and relishing this new turn of mood. "One has to wear special gloves when he handles it because hair grows on everything the Stuff touches—on gloves, fingers, clothes. Why, once I spilled two drops on a craggy rock and the next morning (it does its work overnight, y'know) there was a long moustache growing out of every runnel and cranny of the rock itself!"

"Noooo," came from some of the very leprechauns who had ridiculed Larry earlier.

"Noooo," others repeated in disbelief.

"But it's true! I rubbed a bit of the Stuff on the top of my head and the next morning I scarcely knew myself. Hair all over! *Red* hair at that! It grew so fast, I had to have it cut. I tried trimming it with my shoemaker's scissors, but I couldn't do it right. The man never lived who can cut his own hair. So I went to a barber I knew in Ballinaboy and asked if he'd cut it for me. He did—in return for the softest pair of shoes he ever owned—but he swore he wouldn't tell a soul. Was he the one who—?"

"Yes," Danny said. "But you mustn't be too hard on him, Larry. It's too much to expect any mortal, leastwise a barber, to keep such a juicy story to himself. He didn't *want* to tell it, but I wormed it out of him. Cost me a pair of shoes for his wife and another pair for his mother-in-law before I got the whole thing, but I hung on until I learned it all."

"May I put my hat on now?" Larry asked.

Danny nodded. "But this is an order. No, not an order—a command. When we meet again a year from today, on the thirteenth day of the thirteenth month, you must be as you were, Larry. It isn't fitting for a leprechaun to wear a head of hair. Don't ask me *how*, but you must get rid of the . . . uh . . . Stuff . . . and get rid of that hair, too, even if your banshee friend has to pull it out a tuft at a time!" Then he waved his arms as he always did at the very last and said with more relief than usual, "Meeting's adjourned—till next year!"

From that day on, Larry's life changed. He was suddenly an outsider, an outcast. Everywhere he went, from one end of Ireland to the other, the word had preceded him. It was common knowledge that he had been told to get rid of the wild mop of hair tucked under his pointed hat. His right to privacy disappeared. Total strangers asked outrageous personal questions and pried where they had no right to pry. Once he was wakened from a sound sleep by leprechauns and fairies he didn't even know. They had pulled off his hat, then hidden in trees and giggled at him as the sun came through the branches and made highlights in his thick, red hair.

It is a sorry state of affairs when a body has to guard himself against his own kind attacking him. Truly, the bane of any leprechaun's existence is the constant fear that he will be grasped from behind and held by unrelenting human arms that refuse to let go of him until he divulges the secret hiding place of his gold hoard. The most important lesson a leprechaun can learn is how to talk glibly enough to distract the attention of an attacker for the split second it takes to slip out of arms that have momentarily relaxed their hold. This ever-present human threat was hard enough on Larry's nerves. But the added hazard of never knowing when a preternatural being like himself might slip up on him at any time of day or night was making him positively jumpy.

Larry wandered far from his usual resorts, out of the County of Connacht and past the boundaries of Tara, miles away from the familiar shores of the Sea of Moyle. Sometimes, when he was all alone by a quiet pond and he could be sure that no one, not even a finch or a cricket, was watching him, he took off his hat and warily bent low over the water to see himself. There was always the same excitement when he discovered waves in his hair! Even when the surface of the water was perfectly still, his hair still rippled. And his whiskers, which started at either ear and went under his chin, were no longer a conventional

white but were now a matching red to the hair on his
head. A red-haired, red-bearded leprechaun! As he
studied the water and took in the total reflected effect, he
concluded that he looked at least fifty years younger. He
felt younger, too.

The one disastrous experience with a barber who
couldn't keep a secret had convinced Larry that from now
on he must either cut his own hair or let it grow. He
became adept at snipping the scraggly locks on top and
above the ears, but it was by-guess-and-by-gosh when he
tackled the hair on the back of his head. He awkwardly
reached his cutting hand over his head to snip the clumps
of hair which the fingers of his other hand pinched together. If the result was a bit uneven, he comforted himself with the thought that he looked no worse from behind
that many male mortals who considered it stylish to be
shaggy.

Periodically, he took the untraveled ways home to
check on his possessions. One day he was sitting in his
favorite sheltered place, having a quiet lunch of water-
cress sandwiches, blackberries, and a small potato he had
borrowed from a nearby garden, when he heard a sudden
rustle of leaves and an "A-hem!" Larry saw the shadow of
a fellow leprechaun and jumped to his feet, slamming his
hat onto his head and pulling it almost over his eyes.

"You don't have to do that," his visitor said reassuringly.
"It's only me." Brendan stepped out from behind the
stump of a tree trunk. "Just Brendan stopping by for a chat
and a bit of a favor. Where have ye been, Larry boy? I've
looked here for weeks and it's been totally deserted."

"I tried to run away," Larry confessed. "But I had to

come home again." He knew he didn't have to go into his homesickness for the smells and sights and sounds of his beloved Tara because Brendan understood. "How's Danny? Still mad at me?"

"Danny's not mad. The awesome authority of being in charge makes him sound unfeeling, but he's not unfeeling at all. Why, Danny's like me own grandson. It's partly because of him I've come here every day to look for you. He's worried that maybe he was too harsh in the way he spoke to you in front of everybody at the yearly meeting. When I make my report to him, he'll be happy to know you're home again."

"And Tommy?"

"Turned over a new leaf, he has. No complaints at all about his chewing unreasonable bits of gold from peoples' coins."

"And Patrick?"

"Scratching away." Brendan sighed. "Patrick doesn't need an itch for an excuse to scratch."

Larry was touched by this visit from his friend. Then he remembered Brendan's greeting. "Did you say you wanted a bit of a favor? I hope I heard you right. I'd like to do something for you, Brendan. Name it."

Brendan looked carefully to the right, then to the left. Then just as carefully to the trees above and the rocks below. Satisfied no one was near, he stepped closer to Larry and barely whispered, "Have you still got the Stuff?"

"I have. In a manner of speaking it's within arm's reach of where you're standing."

"Then could you show it to me, Larry lad? And could

you spare just a drop of the Stuff to make old Brendan happy?"

"You can have as much as you wish," Larry said. "But are you sure you want a head of hair? It might grow in red like mine, or even yellow or green. Then you'd be different, too, and the others would hurt you as they've hurt me."

"Not for me *head*, boy. 'Twould be too obvious. No, not the head, but. . . ." He came even closer and made his voice so soft that not even a tree fairy could eavesdrop. "It's me chest. I've never had the sign of a hair on me chest. D'ye think the stuff could grow a little there? The color makes no difference. No one will know but you and me."

"Happy to oblige," Larry said, beckoning with his forefinger as he led the way to a great old tree, thousands of years old, with roots that came up in ridges all around its base. The moss on the ground around the tree seemed to be incredibly thick and shiny, and then suddenly Brendan observed that it wasn't moss at all. Nor was it fern, nor lichen. It was—hair! He pulled at Larry's sleeve and pointed to it.

"I know. I try to be careful but sometimes a teensy tiny bit of the Stuff gets on the ground—and it grows hair there, too."

Larry put his hand between two roots, then reached back almost to his arm's length and slowly pulled out the bottle. "See? Even though I corked it tight, a bit of the stuff seeped onto the glass." Sure enough, long hair was growing on the bottle itself.

Larry reached between two other roots and found a pair of gloves with thick patches of hair on them. "Now!" he said professionally. "Show me where."

Brendan's fingers trembled as he unbuttoned his green jacket and lifted his undershirt. "Here," he said, revealing his smooth white chest.

Oh so painstakingly, Larry uncorked the bottle, poured two drops on Brendan's chest, then corked it again quickly and put it back into its hiding place.

Brendan kept staring at his chest as though he expected immediate results.

"It takes overnight," Larry assured him. "Tomorrow morning you will have hair on your chest. Come here first thing. I'm curious about the color."

Sure enough, Brendan was back early in the morning, unable to control his excitement. He had forgotten his undershirt the day before, so he had only to unbutton his jacket to show what the Stuff had produced. His chest was thick with tiny ringlets of hair—not coarse nor stiff, but soft and silky—and the color, to his ecstatic delight, was as gold as the gold in his crock of gold. A golden miracle!

Larry detected new stirrings within himself. When he tried his hand at the old skill of shoemaking his fingers got clumsy, causing him to drop tools and miss stitches. Worst of all, he found himself drawn toward people. Where, in the past, he had avoided human beings at all costs, he now gravitated toward pageants, assemblies, and fairs where large numbers of people congregated.

First he traveled to that epic of madness, the Donny-brook Fair. He hid himself conveniently there under a wagon used by would-be entertainers as a dressing room and dormitory. He felt sorry for the shabbily costumed dancers who couldn't dance and comedians who weren't funny as they tried to compete with the shouts and curses of drunken, quarrelsome spectators. Sometimes their acts were suspended altogether while members of the audience cracked each others' skulls with whatever was handiest: shillelaghs, clubs, or fists. Donnybrook!

Next, he took in Puck Fair in County Kerry, then the Wexford Operafest,and then he even visited the great Dublin Horse Show which exists on such a refined and dedicated plane that it is as much a spiritual experience as it is a look at horseflesh.

Why this craving for crowds and celebrations? It undoubtedly had something to do with his hair. He had been taught from birth that humans were his enemies and would show him little mercy if they caught him, yet the hair-consciousness he now shared with people seemed to draw him to them.

Were those jeering lurikeens at the council meeting right, after all? Was he, indeed, as odd as two is even? To make things worse, word had filtered out to Irishmen everywhere that there existed a red-haired leprechaun who possessed a sure cure for baldness. Old and young dreamed of catching the little fellow and forcing him to hand over the bottle of magical Stuff that would make the finder richer than a dozen crocks of gold!

It was on a racing day at Listowel that Larry came within a whisker of losing his mind, his honor, and his precious Stuff.

Listowel is forty miles from Limerick, but the difference between them is greater than the distance. Listowel is a healthy, country-bumpkin of a town, totally different from its urban neighbor. There's a proud old church in Listowel's village square, and less than two dozen steps away from it, you'll find the crumbling wall of an ancient, pagan castle. Cobbled streets radiate from the square like spokes from a wheel. Listowel is so sleepy and slow-paced most of the year that one wonders how the many shops and pubs that front on the cobblestones do enough business to keep their doors open. But at Fair time Listowel explodes. It becomes a lusty, gusty, push-and-shove maelstrom of tinkers and grifters and beggars and farmers and sightseers and race visitors. The crowds are so thick in the pubs that drinks have to be passed hand-to-hand from the bar at one end to the front door at the other. Carnival folks set up open-air concessions in the square itself, and here the unsuspecting farmer learns too late that the hand is quicker than the eye and the pod is always under the wrong shell. Citified people, some from as far away as the United States, are drawn to Listowel at Fair time and no wonder: a wild and wonderful recklessness takes hold of native and tourist alike. Horse racing every afternoon for four days, dancing in the streets every night for four nights. The Listowel Fair extends all the way from Listowel to Ballybunion. The wildness is unbelievable.

The River Feale is the rim of the wheel that circles Listowel. Its current is swift, its rapids dangerous, its water icy cold. Larry's moment of truth was destined for the bank of the River Feale.

Arching like a small rainbow across this frigid stream is

a narrow stone footbridge built a thousand years ago by
one of the conquerors of Ireland, perhaps the very one
whose crumbling castle wall still stands within the square.
Modern concrete supports reinforce the bridge at either
end, but the bridge itself is hopelessly narrow, too narrow
by a thousand years to accommodate the throngs that
inch their way across it to the green and spongy turf
bordering the racetrack on the other side. Some of the
revelers pause long enough to toss coins over the side of
the bridge at children wading in the nippy waters below.
Once across, and then a hundred steps farther along the
uncut meadow grass, in the very shadow of the ancient
grandstand, a trio of tinker musicians (fiddle, accordion,
harmonica) stand behind a weathered piece of carpet,
playing lively jingles while the rug fills up with money.

Larry was listening to the music, too, but nobody knew
it. He had hidden himself under the bridge in a spot where
he could share the excitement of the amiable race-goers,
while enjoying a shelter from the sudden gusts of rain
which alternated with the moments of sunshine.

Here on the riverbank, under the darkest end of the
arched bridge, Larry felt secure. He could even catch the
sound of the horses as they rounded the end of the turf
oval nearest him and he could hear the crowd roar its
encouragement as the horses approached the race's end.
He approved the Irish custom of cheering a winner,
whether or not you had your money on him.

Larry knew that nobody in his right mind would leave
an Irish racetrack until the last horse in the last race had
crossed the finish line, so he allowed himself the luxury of
removing his shoes and stockings and dipping his toes into

the clear, cold water of the river. Then he took off his hat, gave his head a shake, ran his hand through his hair, and admired his reflected crimsoned image in the quivering water.

Caught up in the excitement, he lost track of time. He was startled when the tinker music began again. The racing was over. Sure enough, lucky bettors who had made a wish on the tinker music going in to the track were openhanded with part of their winnings as they headed home. Larry put on his shoes and stockings as quickly as he could and crouched low in his hiding place among the shadows under the bridge.

In a matter of moments, 15,000 people were trampling and bruising the long, green grass again as they funneled their way toward the tiny bridge. Since the bridge could accomodate just so many and no more, a surplus of would-be crossers soon began to spread out like an apron over the meadow. Since there was no shorter way to get to the other side, one simply had to suspend all forward movement there near the entrance to the bridge and wait his turn, applying to those ahead of him the same degree of pressure that was being applied by those behind him.

A few of the young men, overexcited by the music and shoutings (and a Guinness too many at the refreshment stand), refused to huddle with the others and wait their turn at the bridge. Instead, they left the crowd, scampered down the slopes to the river itself, took off their shoes and socks, and waded into the icy rapids of the stream. They whooped and hollered like wild hyenas as they splashed across the river, defying its current, and clambered up the steep bank on the other side.

Larry, terrified at being discovered, crept up and up to the darkest part of the bank, where the foundation stones of the bridge had been set so many centuries before.

And then he saw the hat, *his* hat, right where he'd left it by the bank of the river. In his rush to scramble out of sight, he'd foolishly forgotten his hat and he knew too well that whoever found a leprechaun's hat would search everywhere for the owner. Without pausing to weigh the worth of the chance he was taking, Larry crept the few feet to the hat, grabbed it, and darted back.

Too late.

A shaft of light from the setting sun caught and held the intense redness of his hair at exactly the instant that a husky lad in his late teens was sitting alone by the river, removing a shoe. The quick Irish mind, sharpened by the noise and confusion, sensed immediately who Larry was, and the boy made a dive for the red-haired leprechaun.

Trapped, by the water on one hand and the mob on the other, Larry felt the strong arms encircle him. Wriggling desperately, Larry almost managed to elude the grasp and slip away—and he would have succeeded in doing so but for his thick, long hair. His tackler grabbed a handful of hair and held Larry that way until he could grab him by the shoulders, this time for keeps.

"I've *got* you!" the lad exulted. "I won't let you go till you tell me where your Stuff is hid!"

Since the struggle was taking place in the shadows under the bridge, the antagonists were concealed from the people on the bank directly above them. The shoving and pressing to get onto the bridge was a struggle on another level from his own struggle, and Larry's only chance of escaping depended on those above him remaining unaware of his predicament below them.

"W-what s-stuff?" Larry stuttered.

"Sure and you know the stuff I mean," the strong one growled into Larry's ear. Still panting for breath, his captor kept on talking. "The magic Stuff that makes hair grow. I'll sell it by the drop to bald men who'll pay good money for it. Tell me before I crush you. Where is it hidden? Dare to try a leprechaun trick on me and I'll break your arms!"

Instinctively, Larry summoned his cunning and his conditioning. He stopped struggling, went limp in the other's arms, and said dejectedly, "You win! The Stuff is in a flask inside my coat. Loosen your hold a bit, and I'll give it to you."

"Oh, no, you won't!" said the grappler. "I'll reach for it meself." Too greedy for sudden riches to see through Larry's strategy, the foolish one unclamped his victim long enough to push his hand under the green coat.

That one, unguarded second was all Larry needed. He sprang alive, squirmed free, and butted the surprised and furious human so hard in the midriff that he caused him to lose his footing and tumble backward into the cold water.

Surprisingly calm in the face of such a close call, Larry picked up his hat, pulled it down on his forehead so it would not fall off, then ran up the bank to the underside of the bridge and proceeded to pull himself, hand-over-hand, all the way across to the other side.

The lad he'd tricked, still dripping wet, was on his feet now. He was waving, yelling, and pointing to the bridge where he, and only he, could see the tiny leprechaun swinging his way to safety.

"Stop 'im! Stop 'im! It's the red-haired leprechaun!" The frustrated boy screamed as he pointed to the green monkey scooting hand-over-hand underneath the bridge.

But his shouts were lost in the noise of the crowd, packed together like sheep at branding time and totally preoccupied with inching its way onto and over the narrow bridge. A few of the crossers looked over the bridge railing and saw the frenzied young man below them pointing and shouting, but since they couldn't hear a thing he was saying, they just waved back at him in a friendly way.

"Stop 'im before it's too late!"

But it was already too late. Larry had lost himself in the reeds on the other side of the river, and still trembling, was concealed under a large willow tree, where he proceeded to rub his aching arms and sigh with relief.

Slowly, with meticulous care, Larry made his way back to his Tara home on Lake Corrib. He traveled at night, spending most of his days applying dandelion poultices to his muscles, which still ached from his overarm escape under the bridge supports. Finally, at three in the morning of the third day, he stood before his tree, checked the bottle of Stuff and the special Stuff gloves, and found everything as he'd left it. Then he wedged himself comfortably between two gnarled roots of the old tree and slept without stirring until midnight.

When he awakened, he gathered a few berries and crushed some mint for a hasty snack; then he set out to find a nearby castle where the aged owner, a nobleman who traced his lineage back for at least fourteen generations, was at that moment preparing to leave this earth for the kingdom of his ancestors.

Larry kept listening for the cry of the banshee and he was still some distance away from the castle when he first heard the mournful sound. It pulled him in the right direction, like tree markings on a trail. In less than an hour he could see the banshee, tearing her hair in grief and lamenting in the fashion of ancient mourners.

"Deirdre," he called.

He knew she had heard him, but she showed no sign of recognition.

"Deirdre," he repeated. "It's your friend, Larry. I need to talk to you. Will you come to my old tree when the sun comes up?"

She nodded but continued her keening, so there was nothing to do but return to his base and wait for her.

As she slowly approached the tree, she looked pinched, exhausted, and strangely beautiful. He offered her some berries and a bunch of seedless grapes he'd borrowed during his Listowel visit. While she ate them, he asked, "Does your leg bother you much?" He remembered how deeply the trap had cut into her flesh.

"Only when it rains," she said. "You were a good doctor, Larry."

What a contrast, he thought, between her recent tragic wailing and the soft voice that answered him now.

"I am trapped, Deirdre. "I want to give it all up: the bottle of Stuff . . . and the gloves . . . and . . . ." He choked on the last words, "And my hair."

She reached over to him, touched his hand, and ran her fingertips lightly along the contour of a curling red wave. "What a pity," she sighed. "It's such pretty hair."

"Yes, but it has made me miserable. The other leprechauns think it's silly, and Danny-the-Leader decrees that it must go. Oh, Deirdre, I liked having hair because . . . because it made me feel *special*. I possessed something uniquely my own." Without being aware of it, he had spoken in the past tense, as though the hair were already gone. "But people won't let you be special, even if you do them no harm. They point their fingers at you and say things such as 'He's as odd as two is even.'" He touched his hair. "I'll miss it, though. It warms my head on cold mornings. It shields me from the sun. I'll miss it very much—especially when I look into a quiet pool and see myself reflected there. I'll—I'll look like everybody else again."

There was gentleness in Deirdre's eyes as she said, "Most of us go through life missing things we've known and lost. You are no exception. Relinquishing what one loves is as much a part of living as living itself. How empty it would be to grow old and never miss anything." She was lost in her own thoughts for a spell, then she shook her head and returned to specifics. "Get the Stuff and bring it here."

Larry went to the secret place, put on the special gloves, lifted out the bottle of Stuff, and set it before the banshee.

"How . . . how will you do it?" he asked. He flinched when he remembered what Danny had said about pulling it out a tuft at a time.

"It's really very simple," Deirdre said, picking up the

gloves and the bottle with no fear at touching them. "Leave it to me. My friend, you will be bald again, and you will conform, but I promise you that you will *not* be like everybody else. You will still be a very . . . *special* . . . leprechaun. Only you and I will know how special you really are." As she said this, she kept making slow circles with her left hand while staring into Larry's eyes. In half a minute she had hypnotized him into the deepest of sleeps.

The first thing Larry did when he awoke was feel the top of his head. Smooth and hairless it was. He ran to the edge of Lake Corrib, hesitated, then peered into the water. Bald. It had been such a sound sleep that he began to wonder if he had dreamed it all, dreamed everything. In the sunlight the very idea of hair on a leprechaun's head was ridiculous. Had it all been a dream?

He walked slowly to the tree and examined its roots. Only velvety moss was there; the hair was gone (if, indeed, there ever had been hair!). Then he walked over to the craggy rock with the moustache. The moustache was gone, too.

He expected to shiver a bit as he usually did from the coldness of the bare rock when he perched on it, but to his surprise he found it agreeable. He touched the rock again to be sure. It was damp and rough and clammy cold, yet he felt both cushioned and warm with it under him.

An unbelieveable premise occurred to him. No! It *couldn't* be. He walked into deep shadows behind the big tree, where no one could possibly see him, and did a quick bit of exploring. The premise became a fact and a reality.

The hair from his head was gone, all right, but it had been
. . . had been. . .

"Transplanted!" he said aloud.

It wasn't a dream, then. Deirdre's words had meaning
now: "Only you and I will know how special you really
are."

How thoughtful of her! Now he could sit on the frostiest
ground without wincing. And this secret gift would do
wonders for his rheumatism!

Never again would any one call him as odd as two is
even. He wasn't odd. He was *special*. He got out his
shoemaking tools and worked through lunch.

The Toecatcher Christmas

The Toecatcher Christmas

"Toecatcher" isn't in the dictionary, but it should be. The word says exactly what it is, and once you hear it, you'll keep it in your vocabulary forever. If there were a formal definition it might read like this:

> Toe · catcher (tō · kach′ ər) *n.* A useless or almost useless object which has been received as a gift. (1) A what-is-it which the recipient keeps well out of sight. (2) A useless gift which is sometimes kept on the floor of a closet or storage room, causing people to stumble over it. (3) Anything that catches one's toe by mistake.

A cheese tray in the shape of a wheelbarrow with knives for handles is a toecatcher. Crocheted hangers are toecatchers. A forty-hour candle in an oversized setting of malachite-patterned stalactites and stalagmites (shaped underwater for perpetual clamminess) is a toecatcher. A door knocker made of brass and painted in three colors with the word Shalom under the knocker and *Made in Japan* on the back is a toecatcher. Things like that.

This is the story of George Thompson, the first man in history to do something about toecatchers. George was a successful insurance man who surely must have sold the first hypothetical icebox to the first hypothetical Eskimo. George conceived what he later called "the most daring sales plan of his life" when he decided to sell his own family on the idea of giving away their old, accumulated toecatchers as Christmas gifts.

It had bugged George for years: the eternal question of *who gets what for Christmas*? Millions of Americans like himself wrestled with the problem every year, and it was getting worse instead of better. George liked to think of himself as typical. And wasn't his family typical, too? Father, mother, grandmother, daughters aged fifteen and eleven, son six. He'd seen them all knock themselves out to select the right presents for people on their Christmas lists, only to be disappointed when those same people selected the wrong presents for them. The upstairs cedar closet, the basement utility room, and heaven knows how many drawers were packed with these Christmas mistakes.

It wasn't the money involved, George kept telling himself, it was the principle of the thing. But on reflection he had decided that it was the money, too. If the family was going to England and Ireland next summer, they could use the Christmas-present savings to buy souvenirs to bring home. The trip was to be his own Christmas present to Alice, his wife, the children, and his mother, and while he hadn't told anyone yet, it was all but definite. He did some figuring in his head. Using the old toecatchers as a nucleus, they could work from there and augment the on-hand gifts with whatever new came in this year. The saving would be considerable.

Like a general who has memorized his battle map, George knew where his strength and his weakness lay. He was reasonably sure he could count on his mother and the two younger children to side with him because his mother usually sided with him anyway and Roberta and Tommy liked games. Susan, his oldest, was at the opinionated age and she'd be the first to find flaws. And Alice? He couldn't be sure which way she'd go, and Alice was the key figure who could either make or break the whole thing.

Knowing from his years of experience in the insurance business that most people automatically resist new ideas and that the right timing is vital to any presentation, George was careful about when to announce his plan. He chose the Sunday before Thanksgiving, during Sunday dinner, and as it turned out, he eased into his idea during the soup, argued it during the roast chicken, and wrapped up the sale during the egg custard.

"Don't get me wrong," he began. "I love Christmas. I really love it. I love the Christmas *spirit*. But I don't like what people have done to it. They've commercialized and materialized it to the point where the very thought of choosing Christmas presents is depressing. Gift-giving has become a chore instead of a pleasure."

Alice wondered what George could be leading up to. She didn't underestimate his ability to sell something, whether it be an insurance policy or a new idea. She noticed that Grandma Thompson had left the room the minute she had finished her dessert. That wasn't unusual because Grandma Thompson's attention span was zero and she was forever in and out, up and down, here and away, as busy as a hummingbird. Then Alice caught Tommy's eye, pointed menacingly at his untouched custard, and waited to hear what George was going to say next.

"So why don't we *do* something about this situation we've got ourselves into? By *we* I mean we, the Thompsons. I propose that we rebel against gift-giving merely for the sake of gift-giving and substitute—" He dramatized his clincher by scraping his spoon energetically against his empty custard dish in a futile effort to salvage one last half-bite. "—Swapping for shopping."

Alice carefully replaced the spoon with her uneaten bite of custard on it back onto the dish. "Swapping for *what*? You mean . . . we won't buy presents for the people on our Christmas lists?"

"Right! We won't shop for others. Only for ourselves!"

Alice didn't know how to phrase her question. "Isn't that being selfish?" she suggested.

George gained a minute before he had to answer because Tommy, who had eaten two small bites of his custard, began a whole series of sneezes. Alice mechanically produced an allergy pill, mumbled something about how convenient it was to blame it on allergies if you didn't like something, and looked at George again.

"There's nothing selfish about it," George continued. "We'll give presents as we always do. We'll buy for each other as we always do. But to everybody else—well, we'll give unto others what others have given unto us." His eyes were twinkling exactly as they did during the high point of a sales pitch. "We'll give the things we've had around here for years . . . plus whatever comes in this year, that we don't want. It'll be a no-sweat Christmas."

"A no-*what* Christmas?" Alice asked, but not derisively. Pleasantly, in fact. "No-*what?*"

"No-*sweat*. In other words, an *easier* Christmas. Just think: we won't have to fight those crowds of Christmas shoppers. We'll save time and we'll save trouble. Money, too." He added the last two words as though they were an afterthought and pretended he didn't notice Alice's sudden frown.

"But Dad-dy," Susan expostulated, in the tone fifteen-year-olds use when expostulating to utterly silly fathers. "What if we don't get anything *giveable?* I'd just *die* if somebody didn't give us something that looked like . . . Well, like *Bobby!*"

"Bobby?" George could have bitten his tongue for the way he pronounced the name. There was something about Bobby that made George lose control. Bobby was almost sixteen, angular, a perpetual grinner, the possessor of a stomach that was a bottomless pit. Also, Bobby's voice cracked like broken glass when he said, "Thank you, Mr. Thompson, for driving us to the dance." George detested Bobby. He forced a more conciliatory tone, however, and asked, "What were you planning to buy Bobby? Cuff links?"

"Don't you remember? I gave him cuff links last year."

"A duffel bag? You might as well know, Susan, that men have little use for duffel bags." Bobby was most certainly not a man in George's books, but he had been promoted to manhood from his status of whippersnapper in the name of salesmanship.

"Bobby already has three duffel bags."

George knew he had to win this first skirmish or the battle was lost. "After-shave lotion?" There was a sudden vision of Bobby, fully lathered, scraping off the grin with the fuzz.

"Bobby hates perfumy-smelling stuff," Susan announced possessively.

"So here's the perfect answer," George continued, unleashing all his sales power. "Uncle Jake sends me a twelve-dollar necktie from New York every Christmas. Stripes. I don't go for stripes—but I'll bet Bobby loves 'em. I hereby guarantee you Uncle Jake's twelve-dollar striped necktie for Bobby the minute it arrives. OK?"

"A necktie?"

"*Stripes!*"

Susan suspected her father was using his think - of - your - destitute - family - if - you - don't - pay - the - first - premium - on - your - insurance - this - minute technique on her but she couldn't come up with a single logical rebuttal to his reasoning.

Tommy started another siege of all-too-familiar sneezes.

"Eggs," Roberta said knowingly. "Every time we have custard Tommy sneezes."

"It's emotional," Alice announced defensively. "He hates custard."

"Worse than that, Mother," Susan said, "if you were six years old and suddenly saw all your Christmas presents going out the door, wouldn't you sneeze, too? Tommy doesn't like Daddy's idea."

"That's not *so*," Roberta flared. "Make her take that back, Mother! Susan's just mad about having to give Uncle Jake's necktie to Bobby." (George congratulated himself on figuring one thing correctly: since Susan had been less than enthusiastic about Daddy's proposal, Roberta was gung ho for it.)

"Surely Daddy isn't ruling out Santa Claus?" Alice ventured, reaching for Tommy's unfinished custard and placing it in front of her husband.

Tommy began to take a new interest in the discussion. "Santa Claus?" he asked. "Is something going to happen to Santa Claus?"

"Of course not!" George said, secretly relieved that Alice hadn't already put thumbs down on the whole plan. "Santa Claus is still coming down the chimney, Tommy. He'll still have gifts for all of us, the way he always does. And we'll buy each other presents the way we always do. We just won't have to worry about buying things for Uncle Jake, the Martinsons, the O'Haras, Uncle Ben and Aunt Ellie, Cousin Jack, Mr. Harrington, the postman, the paper boy, teachers—people like that."

"You forgot Bobby," Susan said indignantly.

"And Bobby," George said. (Who could forget *Bobby*?)

Alice could feel George's eyes on her, searching for a clue that would tell him if she was for or against his revolutionary proposal. To tell the truth, she couldn't make up her mind. The old system had its drawbacks but it worked. George was proposing a plan that could conceivably backfire. The horrible thought of giving the same toecatcher back to the person who gave it to them originally made her flinch. She looked at George. He had the same happy look that he had worn when he brought home the Runner-Up Cup in the All-City Golf Tournament. "I played over my head," he had said then. "You know and I know I'm not that good a golfer." Maybe he was playing "over his head" now, too. Alice decided to say nothing for the time being. Sometimes, if she just kept still, George blew himself out and nothing came of his brainstorms.

George finished Tommy's custard, stood up, and said, "Let's go to the clubroom for a short family conference. I want to hear my mother's opinion."

Susan always called Bobby as soon as Sunday dinner was over and tied up the telephone for hours. When she heard her father's announcement of a family meeting, she shot him what George called her Bobby-look and said, "Now?"

"I promise it won't take fifteen minutes," he assured her.

"That's all right, Daddy," Susan said and smiled.

A funny feeling came over George as he realized how pretty his child was getting, *really* pretty. In the strange way thoughts go beyond words or gestures Susan caught what he was thinking and smiled at him again.

From the moment he had conceived the large room with the fireplace George thought of it as "the clubroom." When Tim Martinson of the district office had helped him become head of his own general insurance agency, George went ahead and added his dream room onto the house (and included a bedroom and bath for his mother while he was at it). Home builders refer to such a living area as a family room, but it was still the clubroom to George. The former living room with its bay window facing the street had become a kind of modern equivalent of the old-fashioned parlor, off-bounds except for special occasions. George's clubroom had been constructed "long enough and wide enough for fifteen couples to dance the twist without bumping into each other," and the fireplace, located at the long end of the room, was designed for "warmth first, looks second." The furniture was well-used, inviting, comfortable. Both couches in the room were for stretching full-length on, and the two slightly soiled wing chairs, facing each other in front of the fireplace, begged to be curled up in. The children did their homework in this room at either end of a mahogany table, so long it needed two lamps. The room would be the perfect setting for toecatchers going out, toecatchers coming in, sorting, gift-wrapping, and packing Christmas gifts.

Grandma Thompson was not one of the talkers of the world. She did her thing through movement. There were times when she approached perpetual motion. Right now, for example, while George was carefully going over everything he had said earlier, his mother couldn't help moving as she listened. She settled herself in her own rocking chair and picked up her crocheting, only to put it down immediately and dash to her room for her spectacles. A half-minute later (while George waited) she was back, sat in the rocker again, rocked three rocks, then jumped up once more—this time to fetch something to cover her shoulders. Her movements were birdlike. She didn't just proceed toward an objective, she whizzed toward it, zoomed, skittered, swooped on it. And when she was especially excited, as she was about what her son was saying now, she seemed to move both up and down and sideways at the same time. At last she sat reasonably still, ostensibly crocheting, but her body seemed to be darting in all directions as her rocking chair moved with the rhythm of her thoughts.

Alice marveled at George's patience. It wasn't easy to be patient with a jumping jack. Finally, he was finished with his briefing. "OK, Mother. That's it. What do you think?"

Grandma Thompson got up from her chair, started to take a step away from it, reconsidered, walked behind the chair, and then decided to lean on it as she said, "There's a mahjong set Aunt Ellie and Uncle Ben gave the family ten years ago. It's never been out of the box. Just gathers dust on the top shelf of my closet. We'll give it to the Martinsons and get rid of it once and for all."

"The Martinsons?" George asked. "Is a mahjong set *nice* enough for the Martinsons?"

"Too nice, if anything," his mother said. "Aunt Ellie spent more on that set than Mrs. Martinson ever spent on a present for us. They always give us something terrible. I'll cooperate one hundred percent if the Martinsons get the mahjong set." She was poised in midair for a second, then ran around her rocking chair and said "Goody" as she finally backed into it.

Alice laughed. Her mother-in-law was right about the Martinsons. Tim Martinson was a nice man and he had thrown a lot of business George's way, but Mrs. Martinson selected their gifts and she had a facility for choosing dreadful presents. Alice's own mother had used the word "toecatcher" for any gift that was attractive enough to buy and give, but not attractive enough to display or use. All one could do with a toecatcher was put it on the floor and trip over it, or store it someplace and in a moment of desperation give it to somebody else. She thought of a few of the toecatchers she was tired of looking at: the set of filigreed pewter wine goblets, the brass fruit bowl that looked corroded if it wasn't shined every time you used it, candy dishes—formless, shapeless, useless—doilies, scarves, a vase in the shape of a violin. The Martinsons were past masters in the art of toecatcher-giving. Not once had they given a sensible, useful, or even truly decorative gift. Most of these gifts were immediately retired to oblivion in the basement utility-room cabinet. Yes, Grandma Thompson was right about the Martinsons, and maybe—just *maybe*—George was right in what he was suggesting. The idea of exchanging old toecatchers for new ones had its merits.

"Then it's all settled," George said overheartily (because it wasn't all settled and he knew it). "Somebody gives *us* something. We give *them* something. And we don't buy *anything* new!"

His audience, with the exception of his mother, was more tolerant than approving. Susan was wondering if Bobby was wondering why she hadn't called him yet. Not one of them was enthusiastic enough to back George up in front of the others.

Any smart insurance salesman will tell you that when a prospect is wavering, but still won't surrender, the salesman needs a gimmick. It's called "finalizing the deal." The more glamorous the gimmick, the better the chance for finalizing. So George reached for his gimmick. "And now for *my* present to the family . . . If everyone is a good sport . . . If everyone cooperates . . . The whole gang of us go to England and Ireland for our vacation next summer!"

It worked. George could see them being gimmicked before his very eyes.

"*Dad*-dy!" Roberta screamed. "That's a *prom*-ise . . . And you can't go back on a *prom*-ise!" She looked at her brother who was beginning to pucker. "No sneezing, Tommy! If you sneeze, we won't go to England!" Tommy unpuckered.

Susan bought it, too. As she hugged her father she thought of Buckingham Palace, the changing of the guard, and perhaps the Queen herself shaking hands with visitors (including Susan Thompson) the way she sometimes did in the newsreels.

George looked at his mother, who was fluttering and flapping with excitement. "Don't you forget, George," she said. "The Martinsons get that mahjong set—no matter *what*!"

He walked across the room to Alice. Her vote was the most important and still the most doubtful. "Well, honey?" he asked pleadingly.

She started to say, "Are you sure *Scotland* wouldn't be more appropriate?" but catching the intensity of his need for her reassurance, she said what he wanted to hear. "It's a deal!"

As Roberta and Tommy cheered and Grandma

Thompson rocked faster and George wiped the disbelief from his forehead, Susan was already draped around the telephone crooning, "Hi, Bobby. *Guess* where we're going on a trip?"

Alice had an easy relationship with her mother-in-law. When George's father had died, it was Alice who insisted that they invite George's mother to live with them. Well-meaning friends warned her of the perils of having a mother-in-law move into her home, but Alice, who had no mother of her own, somehow knew that George's mother would fill that missing place for her and her instinct had proved right. She couldn't have loved her own mother more than she did Grandma Thompson. There was occasional insistence from the strong-willed old lady that she had the means to live alone and should move to a place of her own. Alice knew that these pro-tests were superficial and answered them decisively with (wished for) notes of confidence.

"Who'll help with the housework and the cooking if you leave us? Who'll *talk* to me? And how could I *afford* a baby-sitter half as good as you are, even if I found one?" Alice felt a secret pride in knowing that Grandma Thompson was happier here with them than she could be anywhere else. The nice part was that Grandma Thomp-son knew it, too.

The two of them would spend what Alice referred to as their quiet time each day trading thoughts, planning, gossiping. Then the children would come home from school and scatter the quiet. Alice usually spent her quiet time in one of the wing chairs facing the fireplace, with her sewing basket on the floor near her feet. Sometimes her mother-in-law would sit—or perch—on the facing chair for a brief interval, but Alice was used to her sudden moves, without provocation, in any and every direction. Grandma Thompson invariably ended up in her rocker. It suited her best because it gave her a chance to move and to sit still at the same time.

Nowadays they talked mostly about George's constant repetition that Christmas-giving had lost its original meaning, that most people gave presents because they had to, not because they wanted to.

"At least he's realistic," Alice said, sewing a button on Tommy's shirt. "Yesterday I heard a woman in a bookstore say, 'This books looks just like my sister-in-law, but it's only twelve-fifty. She always spends twenty dollars on my present. Show me something for twenty.'" She finished with the button, cut the thread by biting through it with her teeth, then looked at Grandma Thompson. "Tell me honestly, do you think George's plan is going to work?"

Her mother-in-law nodded vigorously. "Of course it will. Stop fretting, Alice. It's going to be our best Christmas in years."

"Maybe so. Maybe not. But there's one thing sure: it's going to be the most *different* Christmas in Thompson history!"

As though she wanted to dispel Alice's tinge of doubt, Grandma Thompson jumped from her rocker and made a beeline for her room. In no time at all she was lugging back an oversized suitbox filled with lace collar-and-cuff sets, three unopened books (*Christmas on the Farm*, *A Treasury of Inspiring Thoughts*, *Memories of My Indiana Childhood*), three knitted stoles, two magnifying glasses, a paperweight which produced a snowstorm when turned upside down, a framed motto (*God Bless Our Happy Home*), an Irish blessing etched on copper, a green silk telephone-book cover, and at least a dozen more indescribable toecatchers still in their once white, now yellowed gift boxes. "For forty years I've been saving this junk people have given us," she said pointing at her possessions. "Gen-u-ine antiques!" she added contemptuously, "and millions of people buy more just like them every day of the year." She put the things back in the box, trotted to her room with it, and kept right on talking even when Alice couldn't make out what she was saying. When she sat down again, she leaned toward Alice and said almost vehemently, "The thing that bugs me most is that mahjong set. Every time I look at it, I see the Martinsons. Hope they come by on Christmas Day with another of their booby traps. George made that silly rule that says *we* can't give a present unless somebody gives *us* a present first. So for the first time in years I'm actually looking forward to the Martinsons'. Just have to wait, I guess."

"That's the name of the game, waiting. We can't move until somebody else moves first."

Grandma Thompson jumped out of her chair as though she suddenly remembered a cake in the oven, vanished for thirty seconds, then returned holding a black case by its plastic handle. "Here it is!" she said excitedly, placing it on the coffee table in front of Alice. "The box is a real nice simulated leather, and the pieces *look* like ivory, even if they are imitation. Tell me the truth, Alice. Don't you think it's *too good* for the Martinsons?"

"A booby trap for a booby trap," Alice said, shaking her head in agreement. "We've always given them such *nice* presents, and they've always given us such *things*. Now it's our turn."

Alice suddenly remembered how every year Mr. Martinson would mumble an apology for the gift they brought, always blaming it on Mrs. Martinson and always promising that next year he would see to it that the gift was more appropriate—but it never was.

Alice began counting backward: last year the Martinsons had given them a brown-and-gold plastic valet to hang clothes on. It cluttered a corner of their bedroom for days, insulting the pink décor and giving not the slightest competition to the closet, which was one step away. She had moved it to the cedar closet the morning after George had tripped over it in the dark, hitting his head on the closet door in the process. Two years ago it had been a set of bone-handled knives and forks—two of each. Alice had tried to use them twice, only to have the bone handles come loose each time. She somehow lacked the incentive to glue the handles in place again. The year before that? A "genuine antique" music rack which Mrs. Martinson had "found" at an estate sale.

The year before the music rack? A monstrosity, an undeniable monstrosity. Every time Alice happened to glance at the wall of the utility room, she had to look at it. It was an incredibly abstract, outrageously modernistic watercolor painting, which depicted a streak of red lightning on a solid black background. She found herself subconsciously avoiding the wall where it hung. Mr. Martinson had been especially bothered when they had presented it. "The wife bought this picture at one of those amateur art shows. She says it's pure Impressionism. I say it's pure Rorschach. Hope it makes more sense to you than it does to me." George and Alice had praised it, of course, the way most people praise Christmas presents they abhor, and for two whole days after Christmas the painting dominated the wall of the front hall. To everyone's relief, it was Tommy who forced its retirement to the utility room. Every time he would look at the painting, he would start to sneeze. Alice didn't believe it until she saw the stimulus and response for herself. The picture had as violent an effect on the boy as though the lightning were real and the background his own room. He sneezed, coughed, and showed all the signs of a genuine asthmatic attack. Yes, Grandma Thompson was right. The mahjong set was too good for the Martinsons.

Never before had Alice been finished with her Christmas shopping so early. She had already gift-wrapped Susan's fake-fur coat which, with the portable typewriter and the two new charms for her bracelet, answered all of Susan's hints of the past few weeks. Tommy, who had been so afraid he'd be left out, was ending up with both a sled *and* roller skates, and Roberta's hi-fi set was carefully wrapped in a blanket and hidden in the trunk of their car.

Because she was caught up with her shopping, Alice found herself accumulating extra gifts for the children—a make-up kit for Susan, furry house slippers for Roberta, a

Winnie-the-Pooh record for Tommy. And all simply because everybody in the stores seemed to be grabbing. things, and she had no one else to shop for. The gold cuff links for George (Oh, dear! What had he said to Susan about cuff links?) had been bought way back in October, and her mother-in-law was getting the yarn and pattern she wanted for an afghan.

Alice had discovered a very pleasant dividend from George's toecatcher plan. She liked the closeness that came from their working together, a closeness which included the children and Grandma Thompson—and then, after the others had gone to sleep, a closeness between George and herself, just the two of them. Alice had always loved Christmas Eve, when she and George, like happy conspirators, had put presents under the tree and had worked long past midnight to make everything perfect for Christmas morning. Now it was Christmas Eve every night as she helped George get his "merchandise" ready for the last-minute gift operation.

Two card tables were joined together in the center of the clubroom and equipped with gift papers, ribbons, scissors, and tape to facilitate the quickest of wrapping. After everything was cleared from the long mahogany table, George and Alice lined up unused gifts from the past at one end and cleared a place for incoming gifts (that would soon be outgoing gifts) at the other end.

The children were fascinated with the gift array and spent much of their spare time fingering the assortment of toecatchers, old and new, and making suggestions of possible recipients. One day Tommy looked at the assembled gifts and called them what-is-its. From that moment the table holding them was the what-is-it table.

George pooh-poohed Alice's accusation that he was becoming attached to the toecatchers, but his interest was more than objective. He would fiddle with them —rearrange them, dust, shine, and rebox them— and then stand back and survey them as though they were the costliest of collectors' items. "What an inventory!" he said proudly. "It's better than a department store."

"Or a garage sale," Susan said. When she saw Roberta's dirty look, she added quickly, "A *high-class* garage sale."

For the first time the children could remember, the family Christmas tree was set up and completely decorated ten days before Christmas. In former years it was a case of Mother nagging Daddy to buy theirs before all the trees were picked over, and his finally bringing a tree home at the last minute. Those last-minute trees were almost always too dry, too sparse, too lopsided, too *something*. But this year the Thompson tree had been bought early enough to be fresh and green and full and perfect.

Late one night, while the house and its people slept, George and Alice stood together quietly, admiring the lighted tree. Many of the family gifts were already under the tree and—as a concession to Tommy—Santa would bring the rest as he always did on Christmas Eve.

Now that the clubroom was a part of the house, Christmas was the only season of the year when guests actually used the Thompson living room. The tree was set and trimmed in the center of the room's bay window, so that when it was lighted it was as lovely from the street as it was from indoors. "There are times when I wonder why we have a living room nobody lives in," George said to Alice, "but at Christmas, I wouldn't have it any other way."

"All the ingredients are present," Alice said softly, looking first at the tree, then outside at the bright moonlight reflected as though by a mirror on the snow's icy crust. "Trimmed tree, presents wrapped . . . But something is missing. I've been trying to figure out what that something is and now I know. It's the hurrying, the exhaustion, the fighting the clock to get things finished. Everything is too *quiet*."

"Enjoy the peacefulness while you can," George said prophetically. "It's the lull before the storm."

The initial swap took place at two P.M. on Sunday, December sixteenth, following Sunday dinner. It happened in the clubroom, and it involved a mailing of a gift to Cousin Loretta in Chicago. Cousin Loretta's gift to the family was a set of matching bathroom accessories in a faded, watery blue, a color that seemed strangely unsuited to the black-and-white tile of the upstairs bath or to the all-green downstairs bath or the pinks in Grandma Thompson's bathroom. The set consisted of a bathmat, a toilet-seat cover, and three guest towels, each embossed with a large T. After offering it to Alice and his mother, both of whom shook their heads violently, George placed the set on the what-is-it table and mumbled, "Leave it to

Loretta to put an initial on it. Unless a *T* comes along we're stuck with it."

Cousin Loretta would never know how lucky she was to rate first pick from the collection of toecatchers. Nor would she know that Susan insisted "Cousin Loretta looks like book ends," while George was equally sure "she's the scraggly lace type." Battle lines were drawn. George, Alice, and Grandma Thompson voted for an ecru lace collar-and-cuffs set a great-niece had sent Grandma Thompson from Mexico six years ago. Susan, Roberta, and Tommy held out for the book ends. It looked for a moment as though Cousin Loretta would receive neither (or both), but George won Roberta to his side, stressing the postage-saving by sending the lace set, a saving which would go into the pot for extra luxuries on their trip. Majority ruled.

"It's fun!" said Roberta, who liked the idea of opening Christmas presents ahead of time. "It's like having a whole bunch of Christmases in a row."

"Well, it's *different*," Alice conceded.

Grandma Thompson was all smiles that one of her own toecatchers was the first to be chosen. For six years she had hated that collar-and-cuffs set. Now it was gone forever.

Next to be opened were gifts received so far by the children from friends and relatives. An evening purse for Susan; three Nancy Drews, four records, and two troll dolls for Roberta; a piggy bank, a flashlight, and a box of 100 suckers for Tommy.

Uncle Jake's present to George was next. Susan was at

her father's elbow as he unwrapped it, because this was the famous present for Bobby. George opened the box with confidence, took out the card from Uncle Jake, then handed the box to Susan for the first look. She parted the folds of tissue, gasped, then screamed loudly, "No!" She pulled the tie from the box and dangled it full length. "Look, Daddy! Look, *everybody*! *Polka dots*!"

"Thirty years of stripes, and now Jake double-crosses me when I need him most." George studied the spots. "It's nice material," he ventured. "And it's from Brooks Brothers. That's a good store."

"But Bobby likes *stripes*, Daddy. You know he always wears *stripes*."

"You can tell him to send it back to Brooks Brothers and trade it for stripes. Their address is right on the box."

"That's not *fair*! Mother, you heard him. He promised *stripes*!"

"And you promised to be a good sport!" George said sharply. To his credit, George reminded himself that losing one's temper was no way to make a sale, so he added the word, "Dear." But it had happened. The first hint of moisture had appeared on his no-sweat horizon.

"Be a good sport, Susan," Roberta said, unnecessarily adding her own two cents' worth. "If he doesn't like it, he can send it back."

Susan wheeled on her sister. "And what about the *Arpège* cologne Bobby's going to give me? If we get hard up for a present for some dumb female, I guess I'll have to—"

"Susan!" Sharply again, this time from her mother.

"I'm sorry. But what *about* my *Arpège*? Bobby always

gives me *Arpège* cologne because he knows I adore it. Will that have to go on the what-is-it table, too? Or can I keep it?"

Alice threw a flicker-of-an-eyelash pass at George, which he caught on the goal line. "Of course it's yours to keep, Susan," he said. "And that's a promise."

Susan replaced the tie in its box and patted the tissue folds into place. Then she bestowed a sibling-oriented sneer on Roberta, muttered something about polka dots making a person look *old*, and proceeded to rewrap the necktie for Bobby.

It was a relief to change the subject. "How about this for Uncle Jack?" George asked, holding up the copy of *A Treasury of Inspiring Thoughts*.

"Perfect," his mother said, suppressing a shudder. "And who will be the lucky person to receive Cousin Jack's annual box of candied fruit?"

"Let's send it back to Cousin Jack," Tommy suggested. "If he ever tasted that lousy stuff, mebbe he wouldn't send us any more of it."

"Tommy!" his mother warned. "It's not nice to talk like that. It's Christmas, a time for good thoughts." Alice blushed. Nothing she said sounded the way she meant for it to sound.

George studied the attractively decorated wooden box filled with candied fruits, arranged by color and flavor. Every Christmas, Jack sent them the same box of candied fruit from the same store in Tucson. What a waste of money. It looked so tempting and tasted so oversweet and awful. He thought for a moment about a proper recipient and then he knew he had the right one. "When the

O'Haras cross the street with their beautiful and inedible fruit cake, we'll present them with this gorgeous and vile candied fruit." Nobody disagreed, and nobody doubted that the O'Haras would appear. They always did—and always with one of Mrs. O'Hara's "white fruit cakes," a crumbly confection which tasted uncooked (possibly because it was) and which was glued together with a cheap grade of grape wine for stickum.

"And we'll send the O'Haras' fruit cake to Cousin Jack with the *Treasury of Inspiring Thoughts*," Grandma Thompson said. "He'll get *two* presents this year. Is that too much for him?"

"Oh, let's be generous," George said. "I so move that Cousin Jack get the book *and* the fruit cake." The motion was carried unanimously.

"The gift from Uncle Ben and Aunt Ellie came yesterday," Alice announced. "It's in a huge box but it weighs next to nothing."

"Open it!" Tommy urged. "I'll bet it's a game!"

"Not much chance of that," George said, wrestling with the long, narrow box. "Uncle Ben's and Aunt Ellie's idea of a game is something truly exciting—like musical chairs. My guess is a handworked sampler to hang on the kitchen wall."

He opened the box, peeked, sighed, then announced flatly, "Artificial flowers."

"*Artificial* artificial flowers," his mother said, staring at them.

She was right. They looked sick. There were exactly one dozen of them: three droopy daisies, three limp gladioli, three pitiful peonies, and three anemic snapdragons. Several stems of imitation, waxy, green leaves were tucked on both sides of the flowers.

"All the way from Seattle, Washington!" George said, tracing one of the lifeless leaves with his finger. "Seattle, Washington is famous for everything from canned salmon to pine cones—and what do we get? Petrified posies!"

"Now, now," Alice clucked, trying to sound sincere but not quite succeeding. "Ours not to criticize. It's the thought that counts."

George looked at the box of flowers. "It took a lot of thinking. If someone thought and thought about the one thing the Thompsons need less than anything in the world, he'd come up with these. Want them, Mother?"

As he said it, he turned to where Grandma Thompson had been standing a moment earlier, but she was already at the far end of the what-is-it table where she had snatched a boxed toecatcher and was on her way to him with it. Handing him the toecatcher, she said triumphantly, "Mail this to Uncle Ben and Aunt Ellie special delivery so they'll be sure to get it before Christmas!"

George opened the lid and looked at the two bone-handled knives and the two bone-handled forks nestled in their gray velvet coffin. He lifted out one of the knives, and as he did so, the cutting part slid out of its bone handle. Grandma was up, away, and back again with the household glue. George applied the glue, slipped the cutter into its handle, closed the transparent plastic lid of the coffin, and barked to Susan, "Give it our super-duper, Ben-and-Ellie gift wrap!"

On Monday, December seventeenth, George came

home for lunch, partly because he'd promised to take packages to the post office for mailing, but mainly to see what had arrived in their morning mail. As he and Alice unwrapped the brand-new gifts, they tried to match the senders with appropriate items from the what-is-it table.

An insurance broker from Dallas had sent George a gold-plated shoehorn with a thirty-six inch leather handle.

"I think it's for putting shoes on while standing up," George said sadly.

Alice studied the shoehorn. "Y'know," she said confidentially, "it looks exactly like old Mr. Harrington—and we always send him something. He probably creaks and pops every time he has to bend over to put on his shoes. He might even find it useful. What do you think?"

"Lucky Mr. Harrington."

"And what do we send the shoehorn man?"

George answered immediately. "Nothing. If we give the least encouragement, heaven only knows what he'll send next year!"

An oversized volume entitled A Picture History of Philosophy, from one of George's clients ("he feels he owes me a present because I didn't question his windstorm loss") turned out to be the perfect gift for their minister (after Alice had erased the overlooked sale price inside the dust jacket). The client, in turn, got that old brass fruit bowl from the toecatcher collection. Alice didn't feel the slightest pang of regret as she shined the bowl one last time before parting with it.

George pounced on a package marked Fragile. "Ah,

here's a gift from your sister in Indianapolis. Now ours can go out to her."

"Open it," Alice said nervously.

"*You* open it. She's your sister. I wouldn't deprive you of the thrill."

Alice burrowed into the nest of tissue, stopped suddenly, and groaned, "Oh, *no!*" She reached into the box and removed the vase, holding it up for George to see. "I don't believe it! Mary's sent us the very vase we sent her two years ago!"

George grinned. "*See?* We're not the only ones. . . ."

"But we're not returning the *same* gifts. We're careful about that. Mary ought to be ashamed. Your mother's been after me to send Mary those filigreed pewter wine goblets. I didn't think they were nice enough but—" She looked at the boomerang vase. "They are."

George and Alice hummed *Jingle Bells* all the way to the post office. Fortunately, the lines of people mailing unwanted gifts to unsuspecting recipients weren't as long as they had feared, and in less than half an hour they were driving home again.

"Snuggle closer to me, Mrs. Thompson," George said. "Must be ten degrees out there, and this car heater can't cope."

Alice sighed. "This beats a one-horse open sleigh all to pieces."

"Don't get too complacent," he said, putting his arm around her. "I warn you, it's going to get rough toward the last. When it does get rough, try to remember this moment. You and I united against a materialistic world."

"And all the time I thought *you* were materialistic," Alice said, snuggling closer.

"We know our children better, too, since we've worked together on our project, and maybe, just maybe, they've learned something from it. Incidentally, I bought Mother a book of colored pictures of the British Isles, and I'm giving the kids an album of Irish songs. That trip next summer is going to be fun."

Alice didn't move or answer. Her face was hidden in the shoulder of his overcoat.

"Penny for your thoughts."

She stirred. "I was thinking that I'd like to say to you *this minute*, Merry Christmas, darling."

George kissed the top of her head. "I'd like to do better than that, dear, but somebody in the front seat of this car has to make a left turn immediately, and by the process of elimination, I guess I'm it."

The days were bright and bitter cold. The new snow that fell was dry and powdery, and it packed itself tightly against the old. The Christmas shopping fugue crescendoed for all save the Thompsons, who met in the club-room each evening, unwrapped incoming presents, chose outgoing presents from the stock on hand, and played the toecatcher game. Heavy over their heads was the "roughness" yet to come. All arguments (and there were plenty) were settled by democratic processes—even when, as in the case of Tommy's school-bus driver, Alice and George had protested that the gift (a silver-plated cigarette box with matching lighter) was "out of propor-tion." "But we don't *need* them," Tommy had insisted.

"Nobody in our family smokes and, gee, Pete's a swell guy and he'd appreciate them. Besides, he lets me sit in the front seat with him." When Grandma Thompson pointed out that somebody had given the set to George eight years ago and then cast her vote with the three children, George and Alice surrendered.

One of the most surprising developments of the whole experiment was the change in Tommy's attitude. His original skepticism changed to full cooperation once he was convinced that his own Christmas was intact. He redirected his Christmas toys, games, books, mittens, and even the suckers without a protest or a sneeze. He even washed his hands before reading one of the beginning readers prior to readdressing it.

Roberta and Susan kept up with the gift merry-go-round—unwrapping and rewrapping nail kits, hair ribbons, bubble bath, troll dolls, and stationery. Grandma Thompson managed to dispose of the entire suit box full of old toecatchers, while salvaging some "actually usable" presents from the current incoming crop.

"The game is an object lesson in unselfish generosity," George said to Alice, beaming with the first flush of success.

"I'll have to think that over," was all she dared to answer.

Friday, Saturday, Sunday—and then Monday, Christmas Eve. Susan's Sunday School Class included the Thompson house on its caroling rounds. The carolers stood outside the bay window and faced the lighted tree as they sang.

"A Currier and Ives print complete with sound track,"

was the way George described it. Later, when Susan got home ("so cold outside, so warm indoors!"), the work crew, weary from its last-minute labors, shared hot chocolate with her.

Suddenly, packages from each other began to appear mysteriously and find their way to the tree. It was past midnight before George and Alice were certain the children were asleep and that they were free to bring out Susan's coat and typewriter, Roberta's hi-fi set, and Tommy's sled from their hiding places.

"Do I have to brush my teeth?" George asked wearily, after the children's stockings were filled, the lights put out, and he and Alice were finally in their bedroom.

"Skip the teeth," Alice said. "Call it a Christmas present from your toothbrush."

"Thanks. I'll bet I'm too tired to fall asleep."

Thirty seconds later, George was snoring rhythmically. It was Alice whose eyes were open but not only from tiredness. For the first time in her life she had a feeling of apprehension about Christmas Day, and when she finally fell asleep, her dreams were troubled ones.

Christmas morning! A blur of gift papers, ribbons, shouts, hugs, kisses, and music ranging from *The Twelve Days of Christmas* to *Galway Bay*.

George: *"Thank you, dearly beloveds, for the dozen golf balls, the golf shoes, the cuff links, the . . . ."*

Alice: *"Thank you, dears, for the new bowling ball, the slacks, the elegant sweater, the . . . ."*

Susan: *"Thank you, everybody, for the best Christmas ever! Hey! The doorbell's ringing! Someone's at the door!"*

It was Bobby. Dressed in his new Christmas sports coat, he grinned as he handed Susan her present. Looking at him, Susan wondered if her father could be right when he insisted that Bobby grinned in his sleep.

"Hope you won't mind," Bobby said uncomfortably before Susan had pulled the tie-ribbon on the outside bow. "I changed to a different kind this year. Mother said I was getting in a rut."

Susan unwrapped the cologne and stared unbelievingly at the label. *My Sin*. If there was any fragrance she detested, it was *My Sin*. Bobby's *mother* used *My Sin*! Her first impulse was to place it on the what-is-it table the minute Bobby was gone, but she had made such an issue of Bobby's gift that she couldn't swap it for something better now. Her best bet would be to ask the lady who helped her mother at the cosmetics counter if she would exchange it for *Arpège*.

"I was getting in a rut, too." she said. "Open yours."

Bobby looked at the polka dot necktie for what seemed like a long time. "I like it," he said, not grinning. Susan didn't know whether he meant it or not. As for his sending it back to Brooks Brothers, she'd tell him about that when he asked her to the New Year's Eve dance—provided he did invite her.

"Don't forget the New Year's Eve dance," Bobby said, reading her mind.

"If the tie's too hairy, you can send it back to Brooks Brothers and trade it." She changed the subject. "How about some eggnog?"

"Rain check me, please. The folks are waiting. We're going to my grandparents' house." He hesitated, started to claim a Christmas kiss, decided it was too risky, said, "See you later," and headed for the front door.

George, who had gone upstairs, came down just in time to collide with Bobby in the front hall. Bobby picked up his tie box, looked squarely at George, grinned his Christmas Day Special Bobby-grin and said, "Merry Christmas, Mr. Thompson!" It took a great effort on George's part to refrain from mocking Bobby by pulling his own mouth upward with both index fingers in a hideous grin of his own.

After the front door had slammed behind Bobby, Susan walked up to her father and said, "You're winning. I'm losing."

Before George could say, "It's too early to tell," the doorbell rang again. This time it was Mrs. Warner with her twelve-year-old daughter, Grace. Before opening the door for them, George whispered, "Get your mother, your grandmother, your sister, and your brother. It's the Warners. They remembered us and we forgot them!"

Mrs. Warner, a plump woman whose coal-black hair was pulled back in a knot, began explaining almost before she sat down. "For five years we haven't given Christmas gifts, and you folks know why. This year Grace and I decided to remember our old friends just as we used to—before my husband died." She stopped briefly, blew her nose, then said brightly, "Tommy, run out to my car and bring in the basket in the back seat. Be *very* careful with it." While he was gone, she signaled to Grace to hand her some packages. "Here's a scarf and stocking cap I knitted for Roberta. Hope the cap fits. Earrings for Susan. Sweets for everybody." The last was a large box of homemade cookies and candies that had obviously taken hours of work.

Grandma Thompson flew out of the room as though she were jet-propelled.

Alice said to Susan and Roberta, "Come and help me, girls. We'll get some eggnog for Mrs. Warner and Grace." As soon as the kitchen door had swung shut behind them, Alice whispered briskly, "You two run and help your grandmother wrap presents for the Warners. I'll serve the eggnog."

The girls reached the clubroom through the kitchen. There was their grandmother, dancing with the box of artificial flowers as she tried to fit a huge sheet of gift-wrap paper around it.

"Let me help you," Susan said, laying the paper on the table and the box on top of it. "Look on the what-is-it table, Roberta. We've got to give the Warners something else besides these tacky flowers."

Roberta picked up the green silk phone book cover from the far end of the table. "How about this? It's a little frayed on the edges, but it hasn't been used."

"Swell. And can I have that paperweight over there, Grandmother? Or do you want to keep it?"

Grandma Thompson grabbed the paperweight and pushed it joyfully toward Susan. "I've hated it for twenty years. Twenty more and I might get attached to it."

"The paperweight will be my gift to Grace," Susan said. "Roberta, you can wrap the three Nancy Drews and give them to Grace for your gift."

"I . . . will . . . *not*!" Roberta shouted the words. "Those are *mine*, and I'm not giving them to Grace

Warner or anybody else until I've read them. Why don't we give her the perfume Bobby just gave you? I can tell you hate it."

"She could have it in a minute. Honest she could. But whoever heard of giving a twelve-year-old girl *My Sin?*"

Roberta was unconvinced. She made a noise which sounded like *Yaaahhhh*. Susan answered in kind.

Tommy, who had reentered the house with the basket from the Warner car, walked into the living room just as his mother came in with the eggnog tray. Before Alice could serve the guests, Tommy took his basket from person to person, showing off the tiny puppy that slept inside it.

It was an effort for Alice to appear casual. One of Tommy's worst allergies was to dogs, which explained why the Thompsons had no pet. Her eyes kept going back to Tommy, who had lovingly lifted the puppy from its basket and was holding it in his arms. The expression on his face said plainly that this was the greatest gift he'd ever had, would ever have, could ever hope to have. He sneezed five times rapidly.

"Don't you think, dear—?" was all Alice could say to him before Roberta's and Susan's angry voices snapped their way into the living room. Roberta's *Yaaaahhh* sounded ominous enough, but Susan's louder retort sounded even worse.

"George, dear," Alice said, trying desperately to maintain an appearance of composure, "maybe you'd better go and see what's the matter."

When George walked into the clubroom, he found Susan and Roberta knee-deep in gift paper, fighting over the Nancy Drews—Roberta pulling one way, Susan the other. Grandma Thompson was wading helplessly in the wrappings, circling the girls like a referee in a prize ring.

"Daddy, she's—" yelled Roberta.

"Daddy, she's—" yelled Susan.

"*Shut up!*" yelled George, so loudly Mrs. Warner in the living room spilled eggnog down the front of her dress, and Tommy's new puppy started to whimper.

"*Roberta! Susan!*" Syllables of steel. "Do as I say and do it *right this minute* or . . . ."

Instant quiet.

A moment later, Roberta and Susan brought presents into the living room and handed the flowers and phone book cover to Mrs. Warner, and the paperweight and Nancy Drews to Grace.

Later, as the girls and Alice walked the Warners to the front door, Tommy, still holding the puppy and trying not to sneeze, ran up to George and said quickly, "Can I keep it, Daddy? *Can* I?"

Before George was aware of what Tommy was requesting, Roberta ran back into the room shouting, "It's the Martinsons. They're getting out of their car." Then she bellowed, "Grandmother! It's the *Martinsons!* And they've got a *package!*"

Grandma Thompson got Roberta's message and shot out of her room straight to the what-is-it table where the gift-wrapped present was ready. She had waited so long for this moment. Since Thanksgiving she had waited. As the doorbell was ringing, she placed the gift under the tree; then she loped to her chair on the other side of the room, where she sat with her hands folded, breathing hard. By the time the Martinsons had kicked the snow from their shoes, removed their coats, and walked into the living room, she had control of herself.

During the commotion of shaking hands all around, inspection of the Christmas tree by the guests (Mrs. Martinson found what she was looking for), and Alice's returning to the kitchen to pour more eggnog, Tommy had hugged a far corner of the room with the puppy in his arms. When he could stand the suspense no longer, he marched up to his father and asked again, half-offensively, half-defensively, "Well, *can* I?"

"Can you what?"

"Can I *keep* it? Can I keep the puppy even if I'm allergic? Can I?" He carefully placed the dog in its basket, then used a sleeve to wipe his runny nose.

Alice had placed the glasses of eggnog on her best silver tray. As soon as she entered the room, George took the tray from her and began to serve the guests. When he got to Mrs. Martinson, he heard her ask, "What's the matter with the little boy?"

"Tommy wants to keep the puppy. He's never been able to have a pet because of his asthma."

Mrs. Martinson put down her glass of eggnog, went to the basket, lifted the puppy from it, and began cooing to it.

Mrs. Martinson was one of those people born with a talent for doing and saying precisely the wrong thing at the wrong moment. Stroking the puppy possessively, she said, "If you decide you don't want her, we'll give her a good home." She tickled the puppy under its chin and said itchy-kitchy-coo to it in a tone of voice that brought a look of disgust to Tommy's face. Then she stuck her knife in all the way. Holding the puppy tightly, she said patronizingly, "You know you can always come to our house to play with her, Tommy."

To fully understand what happened next, we must look inside the mind of a six-year-old boy like Tommy Thompson. Despite his tremendous efforts at being cooperative about the game, he was being repaid this way. Without even being consulted, he was being pressured into giving away the best present he had ever received in his whole life. (Christmas presents given to him belonged to him, didn't they? If he wanted to give them all away, he could, couldn't he? But if he wanted to keep one . . . just *one* . . . what mean person would prevent his doing so?) In Tommy's eyes, Mrs. Martinson was trying to snitch his pup. Perhaps a vaguely remembered red lightning bolt from the Martinson past was buried deep in his subconscious and it was that bolt which triggered his explosion.

"It's not a *her*, its a *him*," Tommy shouted hysterically, "and he's not yours—he's *mine!*" He grabbed the puppy out of Mrs. Martinson's arms, sneezed three quickies, and then sneezed again. "He's got a good home *right where he is!*" Sneeze.

"Tommy!" from Alice. (*The natives are restless.*)

"Tommy!" from George. (*The natives are running amuck!*)

"He's *my* dog. Mrs. Warner gave 'im to *me*, and nobody's gonna *steal* 'im!" With shocking defiance, Tommy faced both his parents and shouted, "I don't want to play your darned old game any more!"

George wrestled the dog away from Tommy and placed it in the basket. Then, with basket in one hand and Tommy in the other, he yanked both from the room. All the way to the stairs Tommy screamed, "I don't want to be a good sport. I don't want to go to Ireland. I just want my puppyyyy."

Alice started to follow them, but changed her mind and turned back to face the Martinsons. She found it impossible to force herself into an apology because Mrs. Martinson had provoked the outburst, but she had to say something so she said, "I'm sorry."

"Think nothing of it," Tim Martinson said sincerely.

"Too much Christmas for one allergic little boy!" Mrs. Martinson chirped inanely. Alice had the distinct feeling that Tim Martinson was going to hit his wife if she didn't stop talking. "What sort of game didn't he want to play?" she babbled. "He said he didn't want to play the game any more."

Roberta opened her mouth to explain, but Susan's well-placed kick in the shin closed it again.

"I'll ask him that later," Alice said hurriedly. "What he needs now is a nap."

Grandma Thompson could sit still no longer. She jumped up, ran for the package she had so recently shoved under the tree, picked it up, then handed it to her daughter-in-law. "You do the honors, Alice, dear," she smirked.

"Oh, thank you!" Alice said too brightly. "Here's our Merry Christmas to the Martinsons from all the Thompsons!"

"And here's ours to you!" Mr. Martinson said, handing a package to Susan.

Roberta looked at her mother. "May we open it?"

"Of course."

Roberta studied the gift wrapping. She and Susan had a good start on next year's wraps with ribbons and bows that were still fresh, so it made a difference how she opened a package. It was obvious to her, however, that Mrs. Martinson had not only reused these bows and ribbons, but the gift paper itself had been repaired from previous years. So, deciding there was nothing to save, Roberta ripped the ribbons and paper with abandon, lifted out the present, said, "Why, it's—" and stopped cold. Then she sought out her sister. "Susan, come here."

Susan gazed at the gift, her face a study in disbelief; then she parroted Roberta's words. "Why, it's—"

A heavy Thompson silence permeated the room like smog as Mrs. Martinson tore clumsily at Grandma Thompson's gift wrap. She lifted the mahjong set from its wrappings, unsnapped the top, looked inside as though transfixed, idly picked up one of the tiles, replaced it, then slowly looked up, stunned. It was one of the few times, perhaps the only time, in her life that Mrs. Martinson was speechless.

Roberta, Susan, Alice, Grandma Thompson, and Mr. Martinson were staring at her, waiting for her to speak. She finally managed to pinch out two words, the same two Roberta and Susan had used. "Why, it's—"

Tim Martinson did the talking. First he looked at the two mahjong sets, then he looked squarely at his wife and began shouting at her, "*I hope you're happy!*" He pointed at the set she had bought. "You and your Moonlight Madness Sale!" Then, savagely, "I gave you money to buy a waffle iron. I told you to buy a *waffle iron!* But no! You know more about everything than anybody else!"

Before Mrs. Martinson could reply (and from her angry red face, her reply could very well have been a quick toss of the mahjong set at her husband's head), George walked back into the room, smiling happily. "Tommy's sound asleep. We had a heart-to-heart talk. He apologized; I accepted his apology, and we both cried a little, and Merry slept through it all."

"Merry?" Susan asked.

"Merry. That's our new dog's official name. Merry for Merry Christmas. Tommy promises to take his allergy medicine whenever he sneezes. So everybody's happy."

Happy?

George looked at the Martinsons, then at his mother. She seemed to be crying. Not a person in the room looked happy. There was a murkiness in the air—a gloomy, thick murkiness. "What's the matter?"

"Nothing's the matter," Mr. Martinson lied. "We're leaving. Have to make other calls." He paused. "Merry Christmas, George, Alice, Mrs. Thompson, children." It was a brave greeting from a man of good will who was sinking for the third time. Suddenly he looked straight at Alice and said most earnestly, "I *promise* you, Alice, that *next* year—"

Alice interrupted him. "Merry Christmas!" she said as cheerfully as she could. Susan, Roberta, and George chimed in. Grandma Thompson said nothing. She stared at Mrs. Martinson the way some of the disciples must have stared at Judas. As George and the girls walked the Martinsons to the door, Grandma started to rise from her chair but she simply could not make it. Overwhelmed from the shock of duplication, she tried again and sank down again. All her plotting and planning and maneuvering had gone for nothing. *Nothing.* She'd gotten rid of one mahjong set only to get another!

George lingered on the porch a moment, relishing the clear, cold air. He had walked to the car with the Martinsons and then watched them drive away. He wondered if they would ever speak to each other again. Before reentering the house, he did a dance on the doormat, stomping caked snow from his shoes.

Alice sent the girls to the kitchen, then walked into the clubroom where her mother-in-law had gone. The older woman was sitting in her rocking chair in the dark, rocking slowly, her back to the door. Alice went to her, leaned over impulsively, and kissed her on the cheek.

Grandma Thompson acknowledged the kiss with a nod of her head and a pat to Alice's face with her shaky hand. She didn't say anything because she still didn't trust herself to speak. What had happened was in one sense a catastrophe, but in another—and Grandma Thompson smiled in spite of herself—it was insanely hilarious.

As Alice studied her mother-in-law, wavering between laughter and tears, she was reminded of a bowling pin swaying first one way and then another, unable to make up its mind whether to stand or fall.

"It could be worse," Alice said gently. "Imagine being stuck with two of those pesky sets."

"At least," Grandma Thompson said slowly, "the set they gave us is better than the one we gave them."

Alice was so pleased to hear any comment at all that she burst out with, "And this one's not going to become a toecatcher. I'm going to learn mahjong and get a group started. Will you be the first to join?"

"*Me* play *mahjong?*"

"*You* play *mahjong!*" Alice answered positively.

Grandma Thompson got up from the rocking chair, went to the switch and turned on the overhead lights, sat back in the chair, rocked twice, stopped, then asked mischievously, "Why not?"

That did it. The pin fell over. Grandma Thompson had opted not to cry. She began to giggle, then she chuckled, then she laughed. She rocked faster and faster as she laughed harder and harder.

George looked in, thought his mother was sobbing, and made a move to comfort her—only to be motioned away by Alice who was laughing, too. He backed to the doorway, where he stood watching his wife and his mother losing control of themselves.

Grandma Thompson stopped rocking long enough to say maliciously, "Did you . . . (hiccup) . . . see that look . . . (hiccup) . . . on Mrs. Martinson's face when she—?" She exploded again. "It was—*glorious!*"

And now George, too, began to giggle as he watched his mother laugh and rock and laugh some more.

Alice continued to stand behind her, lovingly patting

her mother-in-law on the shoulder in time to the rocking. Both were screaming like lunatics.

After supper, Alice started tidying up with a vengeance. She collected armloads of bruised wrappings and dumped them into a box, which she carried through the snow to the trash can behind the house. George would have done it had she asked him to, but she wanted to do it herself. She straightened the kitchen, then got out the vacuum cleaner and attacked the living-room rug, picking up every bit of stray glitter right to the base of the tree. Then she ran a dry mop over the vinyl floor of the clubroom, shaking the mop carefully into the fireplace where it made sparks fly.

She went to the basement utility room and worked until she had turned a corner of that room into a suitable boudoir for the puppy dog. At the foot of the basement steps she paused, turned around, then went back into the utility room. With the same sureness that marked her bowling movement when the team needed a strike to win, she marched up to the terrible Martinson painting from a Christmas past, took it down, turned it around, and replaced it with its face to the wall. She started upstairs again, reassured now that Merry wouldn't be frightened by that silly red lightning.

Still restless, Alice set tomorrow morning's breakfast table. But there was something else. She sensed that Christmas wasn't ready to be put away, not just yet. Then she knew what she wanted to do.

George was half-asleep on a couch when Alice walked

into the clubroom, shook him, and said, "George, wake
up. Put a fresh log on the fire. And go upstairs and tell
everybody to come down here. Everybody. If Tommy's
asleep, wake him. Your mother's in her room. I'll get
her."

When George asked what for, Alice answered, "For all
of us."

By the time George had rounded up Susan and Roberta
and awakened Tommy, Alice had fetched her mother-
in-law and had the refreshments tray filled. Roberta,
Grandma Thompson, and Tommy (curled up in a corner
of the couch in his flannel robe and house slippers) got hot
chocolate and some of Mrs. Warner's cookies. Susan,
George, and Alice got eggnog, and as she poured it, Alice
said steadily, "This is the last year I'm buying eggnog from
the milkman. Mine's better."

Alice faced her family. She was composed and serene.
"Daddy and I welcome you to our party. We've been so
busy winning the toecatcher game that we've lost the
spirit of Christmas, and that's a pity."

She opened the Bible in her hand and began to read:
*Now when Jesus was born in Bethlehem of Judaea in the
days of Herod the king, behold, there came wise men from
the east to Jerusalem. . . .*

A peacefulness settled on the room as Alice read the
familiar verses from St. Matthew. When she reached the
part: *And, lo, the star, which they saw in the east, went
before them, till it came and stood over where the young
child was . . .* she handed the Bible to George and said,
"Now it's Daddy's turn."

George, touched that Alice had made it sound as

though the party was as much his idea as hers, read slowly and meaningfully: *When they saw the star, they rejoiced with exceeding great joy.*

And when they were come into the house, they saw the young child with Mary his mother, and fell down, and worshipped him: and when they had opened their treasures, they presented unto him gifts: gold, and frankincense, and myrrh. . . .

He closed the Bible slowly and said, "Let's end our Christmas party with a song. Susan, how about starting us off on *Silent Night?*"

It was more than just a song the way they sang it. It was the Thompsons' own Christmas gift to themselves, long past due.

It was after midnight when Alice walked into the clubroom and found George slumped in one of the worn wing chairs that faced the fireplace. He was intent on the occasional flames from the almost burned-out log.

At first she thought he was asleep, so she barely whispered, "Well?"

He moved the facing chair until it was next to his own.

"Satisfied?" she asked, sitting down.

"Well, yes—and no. Toward the last I sweated. Once when we almost ran out of things to swap, and once when Tommy threw his tantrum, and once when Mother killed the Martinsons with that look.

He reached for her hand, and when she held it out to him, he grasped it and held it tightly. "Know what?"

"What?"

"The last part—your part—was the best of all. Those

words we read about gifts. They said it, didn't they? When I read them, I thought of people like Mrs. Warner who give because they want to give, not because they have to. That puppy! It was the realest gift we got." He looked at her and said earnestly, "I think we all learned something about gift-giving. It's not what you give but how you give it. Not *what*—but *how*."

Alice closed her eyes just long enough for a thank-you prayer. Then she said, "Is it too soon to ask about next year?"

"If it's OK with you, Alice, let's go back to the old system and let the what-is-its fall where they may. One more toecatcher year—just one more—and we'd lose the magic of it . . . all the gold, and frankincense, and myrrh. . . ."

She smiled. "It's OK with me."

"I have a confession to make," he said slowly. "That famous trip next summer: I shouldn't have used it as a bribe. We were going anyway. It was to be a surprise Christmas present."

She laughed. "I knew. The travel agency called by mistake, long before you happened to think of it on the spur of the moment, and announced that the reservations were confirmed."

"Well, I'll be—"

He didn't finish the sentence, but he continued to hold her hand tightly as each watched the dying fire.

Neither spoke for what seemed to be a long, long time.